The Lonely Sentinel

The Lonely Sentinel

by
Piet Prins

PAIDEIA PRESS
St. Catharines, Ontario, Canada

First published in Dutch as *Holland onder het hakenkruis,
Voorloper*, © Jacob Dijkstra's Uitgeversmij N.V., Groningen.
Translated by James C. van Oosterom.
Cover design by Chuck Spitters.

ISBN 0-88815-781-9
Printed in the United States of America.

Table of Contents

CHAPTER I

An Enemy and a Friend

School was out. A crowd of boys and girls mobbed the front door. Some of them walked calmly out of the schoolyard while others carried on, shouting and play-fighting, the moment they had escaped the teacher's watchful eye.

A minute or two later the yard was completely deserted. The children had disappeared in every direction.

The only one left was Frans Mulders, waiting by the gate for his younger brother Dirk. He was a little perturbed. His brother had to stay in again!

Frans was in the sixth grade; Dirk, two years younger, was in the fourth. Otherwise they were inseparable. Frans often grumbled about his younger brother, usually with plenty of reason, but when the chips were down he would do anything for him.

Dirk burst out of the school. He laughed when he spotted Frans waiting for him and charged at him.

"It's about time! I bet you had to stay in for not paying attention, right? What kind of trouble did you get into this time?" Frans's voice was stern. He felt called to look after his little brother.

But Dirk only laughed. "Nothing like that! The teacher let me erase the blackboards and help her clean up."

His explanation satisfied Frans and together they started for home.

They didn't look at all like brothers. Dirk was two years younger than Frans, but he was almost just as tall. Frans looked frail. He had dark hair and a rather thin face with dark, thoughtful eyes. Dirk had a much sturdier build, blond hair, rosy cheeks and baby blue eyes that sparkled with mischief. Most people thought they didn't fit together at all, but they were mistaken. They fit together very well, probably just because they were so different.

Dirk was kind of a daredevil, who often leaped before he looked, while Frans was the reflective type. He certainly wasn't afraid, but always tempered valor with discretion. It was a good thing that the impetuous Dirk had a cautious older brother to keep him from doing stupid things. But, on the other hand, it was also a good thing that the somewhat hesitant Frans had a rather more decisive younger brother. They complemented each other perfectly.

It was a stormy, chilly autumn day, and Frans and Dirk were heading straight into the wind. They had both turned up the collars of their jackets. Frans's jacket was worn and tattered. He badly needed a new one, but all textile products were rationed. The German occupation of the Netherlands was already in its fourth year and there was a general shortage of food, clothes, shoes and everything else.

Their mother was a good seamstress who could often do wonders with old clothing, but at last the fabric became so threadbare and tattered that the material wouldn't even hold a thread. Occasionally the boys would complain at having to wear such rags, but Mother always said, "At least be thankful we've got enough to eat! Many people are a whole lot worse off than we are." That would usually put the boys to shame; they knew Mother was right.

The street wasn't very busy. There were practically no cars, because gasoline was available only to people with a special permit. Even bicycles were scarce because of the shortage of tires. The simplest solution was to stay home.

From a sidestreet came the sound of hobnail boots and a German marching song. As the boys approached the corner, a platoon of German soldiers marched out onto Main Street. They were goose stepping smartly and bellowing out martial songs at the top of their voices. After every line they paused two counts before they started on the next.

The boys watched until the platoon had passed. They stared with blank faces. Dirk had difficulty controlling himself. The Germans were the oppressors. Thousands of Dutch people had been imprisoned or taken away to concentration camps. Hundreds had been executed. Freedom of speech was a thing of the past. Newspapers and magazines published only what the Germans dictated. Clergymen who had the nerve to pray for Queen Wilhelmina or speak out against the doctrine of National Socialism ran the risk of being arrested by the German Secret Police, the dreaded Gestapo.

When the platoon had passed, Dirk raised a clenched fist. He shook it menacingly and called out, "Filthy Jerries!"

"Hush!" Frans hissed, but it was too late. Behind them, an angry voice snarled, "What did you say? You'd better come with me!"

Dirk was seized roughly by the neck. He writhed and struggled but was unable to get free.

Frans started at the figure that had suddenly loomed up behind them. He was a heavyset man with a large, pale face and heavy jowls. He was noticeably better dressed than most people. His overcoat was unbuttoned and Frans could see a triangular pin with the letters N.S.B. on the lapel of his jacket. The man was a member of the fifth columnist, pro-Nazi National Socialist Movement.

That shocked him. Members of the National Socialist

Movement were Dutch people who had allied themselves with the Germans. What would become of Dirk?

Dirk was still writhing and twisting; tears of anger and fear sprang to his eyes. Realizing he couldn't free himself from the man's hammy fist he drew back his foot and kicked him hard in the shins.

Dirk's aim was right on and the man yelped in pain. He released Dirk's neck, and Dirk managed to slip away. But the man lunged forward and seized him by the coat. The coat ripped, but not enough for Dirk to make his escape. The man spun Dirk around and grabbed him by the wrist. But Dirk was in a panic now and capable of almost anything. He kicked and struggled again and sank his teeth into the man's hand. Just then what sounded like a shot rang out behind the assailant.

That did it. At once the man released his victim and froze. When he finally mustered enough courage to look behind him, all he saw was the two boys dashing off, the taller one just throwing away a tattered paper bag.

The man immediately realized he'd been taken. The first thing he'd thought of when he heard the bang was that someone from the Resistance had taken a shot at him. He bellowed angrily and started in pursuit. The boys had a jump on him of about thirty meters. They were making tracks as fast as possible. Frans was exuberant that the ruse had worked, and Dirk was relieved to be free. But they heard footsteps behind them, and they could tell that the man was fast closing the gap.

Knowing they would never be able to outrun the man and that he would catch them in a couple of minutes, they looked around for some place to hide. They turned another corner, but their pursuer had just rounded the first one and saw them slip into the alley. They had to hide soon, otherwise it would be too late.

Dirk was almost as strong as his older brother, but Frans was faster. He had to slow down so that his younger brother, already puffing and panting, could keep up with him.

The alley led into a street of high, rundown row houses. Some of the houses had high steps in front of them, and suddenly between two of the steps Frans spotted four green, wooden trapdoors, like those that cover coal chutes.

"This way!" Frans shouted, as he dashed toward the nearest trapdoor. He lifted the hatch, slipped inside, and made room for Dirk. He lowered the hatch just as their assailant turned the corner into the street.

The boys squatted close together in the dark space under the sidewalk. Their hearts pounded wildly from running and from fright. Suppose the man also spotted the trapdoors. They'd be caught like rats in a trap!

They heard footsteps overhead. The footsteps were coming

closer, but the man was no longer running. Apparently he must have started wondering what happened to the fugitives.

Clop, clop . . . He halted right beside the trapdoors.

"Grab hold," hissed Frans. Panic seized him once again, but he wasn't about to give up yet. There were hooks on the bottom of the trapdoors. Frans slipped his fingers through them and pulled down on the hatch for all he was worth. Dirk quickly slipped to the second lid and did the same.

Their pursuer stooped to inspect the trapdoors. The boys could hear his breathing. He grabbed one handle and tried to lift the hatch, but that didn't work. The second one wouldn't give either; that was the one Dirk was holding down. But the man still wasn't satisfied. Grumbling, he stepped to the third trapdoor. The boys inside nearly wilted in fright. The third trapdoor was loose, and there were no hooks on the inside to hold it down. They were goners!

Then a door banged open and an angry voice barked, "Keep your hands off those trapdoors and get out of here!"

For a split second Frans and Dirk thought the man was talking to them, but then they realized it was directed at their pursuer, who immediately dropped the third hatch.

"I'm looking for a couple of little troublemakers and I think they may be hiding in here," the man replied gruffly.

"Do your dirty business elsewhere and keep your hands off my property!" the man at the door called back.

The German sympathizer hesitated a moment. He could easily handle two boys but he didn't feel much like tangling with the man on the front step. Moreover, faces had appeared in some of the other windows, and they didn't look very sympathetic.

He chose discretion before valor. "You haven't heard the last of this, I promise you," he said menacingly, as he turned and walked away. The man on the step only laughed at him. He remained out on the step for a few moments and then went back inside.

Under the trapdoors, Frans and Dirk could hardly believe that it was over. They were still desperately hanging on to the hooks on the bottom of the trapdoors. When nothing happened, they finally let go. Looking around, they discovered they were in some sort of a trench. On one side was a concrete wall and on the other basement windows. The trench ran parallel to the street.

"Let's get out of here and make a run for it," whispered Dirk. He was still worried. But Frans shook his head and said, "No, the coast may not be clear yet. He may be standing around a corner somewhere waiting for us to come out."

"That sure was a neat trick with that bag," chuckled Dirk. "You scared the daylights out of him!"

Despite their predicament, Frans had to laugh. "That was my lunch bag. I thought, I'll blow it up and—Oh, look!"

A face appeared in one of the cellar windows. Piercing eyes stared at the boys from under bushy eyebrows. The man lifted the window out of its frame. "Better come inside, boys. It's safe in here," he said. Frans and Dirk recognized the voice immediately: it belonged to the man who had driven off the Nazi sympathizer. That gave them courage, and they quickly slipped through the window into the cellar.

The cellar was surprisingly large. Stacked on the floor were potatoes, turnips and red cabbages. In the opposite wall was a door which apparently led to another cellar. The man replaced the window pane carefully. He was not a young man, but he was sturdily built and tall enough so that he had to stoop not to bump his head against the joists.

"Well, that was close, boys. You had an anxious couple of minutes there!"

"How did you know we were here?" asked Dirk, astonished.

The man's laughter echoed through the cavernous cellar. "I saw you right away. I had just come into the cellar to get something. I didn't have a light with me because I can find my way around without one. Suddenly I saw daylight coming in through the windows as one of the trapdoors opened. Then I saw two pairs of legs descending into the window well.

"Kids have played in my window well before. A couple of times it's cost me a window. I thought to myself: I'll sneak around to the outside and teach them a lesson. So I tiptoed out of the cellar and onto the front porch. The minute I opened the door I saw the Nazi sympathizer, Dreumel. Everybody around here hates the guy. We suspect him of betraying one of our neighbors who was listening to radio broadcasts from England.

"When I saw that dirty Dreumel fiddling around with my trapdoors, I immediately realized what he was after. So I hollered at him. He backed down because he's really a coward. But tell me, what have you two been up to?"

The boys were no longer afraid; this man had helped them out of real trouble. He didn't look overly friendly, but he clearly had no use for Nazi sympathizers. So Frans told him what had happened. Their rescuer roared with laughter when he heard about the paper bag. But when Frans was finished, the man grabbed Dirk by the ear and said, "You better learn to control that tongue, young man. We all have to these days."

"You weren't afraid to chew him out though," replied Dirk, but at the same time he blushed, because he realized he was being impertinent.

"That was necessary to save your hide. But what you did was just plain dumb. There's a big difference." The man said it very calmly, but something in his tone of voice made Dirk feel ashamed. "What are your names?"

"I'm Frans Mulders, sir, and this is my little brother, Dirk."

"And I'm not sir; I'm Mr. Van Beveren. Mulders you said? Where do you live?"

"Outside the city, close to the mill on the Kanaaldijk."

"That's what I thought! I know your father very well. Give him my regards; we served in the army together during the First World War. Holland was neutral, but we were drafted anyway. That was in 1917."

The man walked to a crate, lifted the lid and gave each of the boys a large Golden Delicious apple. "That's for on the way home. And now let me show you out."

Followed by the boys, he climbed the stairs into a long, bare hallway. Van Beveren didn't bring them to the front door but showed them out the back way. He led them across a small courtyard surrounded by a stone wall and cluttered with crates and drums. The wall was about three meters high with broken pieces of glass cemented into the top to discourage would-be intruders.

In the wall was a door. Van Beveren took a key ring out of his pocket and opened it. Behind the wall was a narrow alley, flanked on both sides by warehouses and other dilapidated buildings.

"Dreumel won't look for you here. Turn right at the next street, that'll take you to the Kanaaldijk. You better go straight home because I'm sure your parents will be worried about you!"

He locked the door behind them. Then it dawned on the boys that they hadn't even thanked him. "Thanks a lot, Mr. Van Beveren!" they called out in unison, but there was no reply.

They walked down the alley like true comrades in arms. When they reached the main street, they stopped to look both ways in case Dreumel was lying in ambush for them.

But the coast was clear, so they turned right and hurried down the street. They didn't say very much. Halting at every street corner to make sure it was safe, they finally reached the outskirts of the city. They crossed the bridge over the canal and then turned left onto the Kanaaldijk. Another fifteen minutes and they would be home. At last they felt safe. At least they didn't have to worry about the Nazi sympathizer anymore.

No longer sheltered by houses, they felt the full force of the wind as it whistled about their ears. It whipped the canal water into foam and howled through the willow trees lining the Kanaaldijk. But the wind was in their backs now. That helped.

Dirk unbuttoned his coat and spread it like a sail so that the wind would blow him along. As he did so, he noticed the large tear in his coat. He couldn't see it very well because it was on his back. "Is it bad?" he asked Frans.

Frans nodded. "Very," he replied unhappily. "Mother may not be able to fix it."

But Dirk was a little more hopeful. "Mother can fix almost anything," he said optimistically. But it put a damper on his high spirits. In any case, they would have to spill everything once they were home.

Frans realized that his little brother was struggling with his conscience; he felt sorry for him. "I'll tell Mom and Dad. When Dad hears that we were saved by an old acquaintance of his . . . well, maybe it won't be so bad."

"Yeah, boy, he really helped us," Dirk said fervently. "If that Dreumel had gotten a hold of us . . ."

"We have to keep our eyes peeled from now on," said Frans. "He'll probably keep looking for us."

The boys fell silent, reaching for the apples Van Beveren had given them. They were getting closer to the mill. It made an imposing silhouette against the dark gray sky in the background—a lone sentinel guarding those who lived beneath its wings. Its arms were still turning, which meant that Father was still milling.

Their house stood right next to the mill. Next to the tall giant, it looked very slight, even dumpy, but it wasn't as small as it looked. Behind the mill was a lumber shed. The mill didn't only grind flour, but it also cut lumber. Behind the shed was a pond with logs floating in it.

"Look, Mother is already looking out for us," said Frans. "She must be worried because it's late." Dirk waved at her and shouted "Hi Mom" as loud as he could. Mother waved back and went back inside. Her two boys were safe, but she wondered why they were so late.

Snippy, a lively black and white terrier, came charging around the corner. He was wild about Frans and Dirk and the boys were just as wild about him. Snip had heard their voices. He ran at them, barked happily and tried to get the boys to play fight with him. But he had no luck this time. Even Dirk, who was usually only too ready to wrestle and play with Snippy, didn't respond. He was thinking about his coat. What would Mother say?

His mother didn't say much, not at first anyway. But later when she saw his coat, tears came to her eyes—something Dirk couldn't stand, because he loved his mother very much. His face turned red and he tried to explain, but he was so upset and confused that he couldn't tell his story straight. "It was all because of those Germans, Mom, and that one Nazi sympathizer—Dreumel was his name—and Van Beveren said—"

"What's the story? How come you guys are so late?" That was their father. He had just walked into the living room, followed by Dries. Dries was their older brother, he was seventeen and helped Father with the milling.

Frans realized Dirk wasn't getting anywhere. "Let me try," he said, and Dirk nodded, obviously relieved. Frans told them exactly what had happened. He didn't hide anything, but tried to defend his little brother as much as possible.

Fifteen-year-old Nel had also come in. They all listened with deep concern to Frans's story.

When Mother learned that her two boys had been in great danger, she forgot all about the coat. Father was very angry because Dirk had been so dangerously careless. He gave him a

severe tongue lashing, but again Frans came to his brother's defense by diverting Father's attention. "Dad, the man who helped us is called Van Beveren. He said to say hello to you. He said you two were in the service together."

That did the trick. His father, who was about to turn Dirk over his knee, wheeled in surprise. "Van Beveren? Yes, that's right, he was my old army buddy during the First World War. What did he say?"

Frans gave a faithful account of their conversation. In the meantime, Dirk had retreated to a corner of the room and tried to blend in with the furniture. But his father paid no more attention to him.

"Good old Janus! I didn't even know he lived around here! I'll have to look him up."

"Did you know him very well?" Frans tried to hold his father's attention as long as possible.

"You bet! Actually, we were a pretty mismatched pair, but he really helped me a lot. I joined up in 1917, when I was pretty young and green. I didn't know from nothing, and basic training was pretty rough. But Janus had joined in 1914, so he was a veteran. He originally came from a district in Amsterdam called the Jordaan. That's not one of your better neighborhoods. Janus was a real inner city kid, always coarse and rough, but he was a lot of fun to be with and a very handy guy to have around. By the time I joined, he'd become a corporal and he supervised our basic training. He could give you a dressing down like you wouldn't believe. But when something went wrong or when somebody was about to be punished, he always stuck by us.

"I don't know why, but for some reason he took a liking to me and helped me through those difficult months. He had no education to speak of, but he was clever and handy and knew practically everybody.

"With the armistice in 1918 I left the service but Janus was a professional and he stayed on. A few years later I heard he'd been shot in the thigh during target practice. He recovered almost completely, but he kept a limp.

"He was given a medical discharge. So he went back to his beloved Amsterdam. For a while he operated a little produce stand where he sold potatoes, vegetables and fruit. But then he disappeared, and I never did find out where he went.

"So he's living here now, is he! I'm going to look him up this week and thank him personally for saving your skins."

This again reminded Father of Dirk, but his anger had ebbed. He raised his finger threateningly and said, "You watch your tongue from now on, young man! You could endanger everybody around here."

Ashamed, Dirk nodded. He looked sufficiently chastened. But he was also very relieved that his father's wrath had been cut short, and he looked gratefully at his older brother.

Mother and Nel set the table. Dirk was immensely hungry. His eyes lit up as Mother came in carrying a large bowl of mashed potatoes and Nel came in carrying two dishes of mustard sauce.

"Go wash your hands first," Mother told Frans and Dirk. Then they all sat down around the table. Father said grace.

While they ate, Father and Dries discussed rumors they'd picked up over the last few days. They kept in touch with a lot of people and were always up to date about what was going on around the country.

Frans and Dirk listened closely. The Mulders usually had no secrets from each other, but they all knew enough not to repeat anything they had heard. Even impetuous Dirk could be trusted as far as that was concerned. Frans often had the impression that Dad and Dries knew a lot more than they were saying, but he wasn't sure and wasn't about to ask.

Today there was a lot of news, both good and bad. The Russians had driven back Hitler's armies past the city of Kiev. Seyss-Inquart, Hitler's viceroy in the Netherlands, had organized a new police force to help the Germans maintain law and order in the Netherlands. Most of those who had volunteered to serve in the new *Landwacht* (National Guard) were members of the N.S.B. Father knew some farmboys who had also joined.

They also mentioned a raid carried out by the Dutch Resistance on a German munitions dump elsewhere in the country. The Germans were renewing their efforts to locate the many fugitives who had gone into hiding. Many fugitives, among whom were Jews, political leaders, and members of the Resistance, had already been captured.

Frans and Dirk knew all about these fugitives. They were usually patriots who resisted Nazification. They were provided with counterfeit identity cards and moved to places where nobody knew them. There were also fugitives who didn't have identity cards, especially Jewish people, and they had to go underground to avoid being caught.

Hundreds of thousands of able bodied men had been instructed to report for work in Germany. Hitler figured that the more foreign laborers he could employ in German factories, the more Germans would be free for military service. Of course, he needed more soldiers all the time, because he sensed that the war was turning against him.

Many did report for work in Germany. By doing so, they aided the enemy, but they dared not refuse. But many others refused to report and went into hiding. Still others reported but were quickly fed up with Hitler's Third Reich and went into hiding the minute they were given a leave of absence.

The Germans, of course, were infuriated. Searching for these fugitives took a lot of manpower, and many of them, aided by the Resistance, succeeded in escaping time and again.

That's what Father, Mother and Dries were talking about, and Frans was listening so intently that he almost forgot to eat. Not so Dirk. Things would have to get a lot worse before he forgot to eat. Besides, he loved mashed potatoes and mustard sauce. He was only half listening; right now eating came first.

"Hurry up, Frans!" Mother said. His concentration broken, Frans attacked his plate of mashed potatoes.

Mother also served a porridge made from ground rye. After supper Father read a portion from Scripture and then thanked the Lord for all the blessings they had received. By comparison, they were richly blessed. A lot of other people were suffering real want. Nearly everything was rationed and supplies were becoming more scarce every day. But the Mulders at least had enough to eat. That was something to be thankful for.

After supper Frans worked on his homework. Since he was only in grade four, Dirk had very little homework. About all he ever took home was a book from the library. Within minutes he was so wrapped up in his book he didn't even notice what was going on around him.

Mother and Nel attacked the dishes. Dad filled his pipe. During the past summer he had grown his own tobacco and cured the leaves in the lumber shed behind the house. It had cost him a lot of trouble and even then it didn't taste like the real thing. But real factory tobacco could only be bought on the black market and prices were out of reach.

Dries, who was taking a night course in bookkeeping, gathered his books together and left for town. It was dark outside. The wind was fiercer than before and black, threatening clouds raced across the sky.

But inside it was warm and cozy. Mother and Nel had finished the dishes and returned to the living room. Everyone gathered around the coal oil lamp. The windows were blacked out with heavy drapes and strips of black paper because it was against the law to show any light outside.

Father took an armful of wood and fed the stove again. Fortunately the lumber mill provided plenty of waste wood because coal was practically impossible to get.

Nel poured coffee, at least, they called it coffee. But it was only a poor substitute—a black, syrupy concoction that was completely undrinkable unless diluted with skim milk.

Dirk was unaware of what was going on around him. In his mind's eye he was in sixteenth century Leiden, surrounded by Spaniards. Everybody was cold, destitute, and hungry. The people had already eaten all the city's cats and rats and tree bark and now there was nothing left. That night Dirk stealthily made his way through the Spanish army besieging the city to deliver a message to the Prince of Orange, who was sick in bed in the city of Delft. The Prince had ordered the dikes cut to flood the countryside. Dirk was sent back at the head of a fleet of flatbottom boats that made its way to the besieged city across the flooded pastureland. They were carrying herring and bread as relief for the starving masses in Leiden. Most of the Spanish soldiers had already fled from the floodwaters, and the rest were driven back by the soldiers in the boats . . .

"Frans and Dirk, it's bedtime!"

Frans, who was already finished with his homework, got up, but Dirk didn't hear a thing. When his mother told him to get going for the second time, he looked up, irritated at being so rudely interrupted. Just when the story was getting exciting!

But then he saw that his mother was trying to repair his coat once more. He blushed. Quickly he gave his mother and father a peck on the cheek and followed Frans upstairs.

CHAPTER II

Rabbits and Traitors

The bad weather lasted several days but eventually it began to warm up. The sun broke through the cloud cover, and although a November sun no longer carries much clout, the weather definitely took a turn for the better.

It was Saturday and Frans and Dirk didn't have to go to school. They played in the lumber shed and the mill all morning. After lunch Frans made a bow and arrow for Dirk. For himself he made a spear from a long, straight willow branch. They were going hunting.

Dirk was sure they wouldn't come back empty-handed; after all, there were lots of wild rabbits in the open fields. Even if they only got one, the hunt would be a success.

They crossed fields, jumped ditches and stalked through underbrush. And, indeed, they flushed plenty of game. Several times they spotted rabbits dashing out of the bushes to safety. It was no wonder there was lots of game: nobody was allowed to own firearms except members of the N.S.B.

They suddenly came upon a beautiful pheasant and, a little later upon a whole bevy of partridges. Dirk had soon used all his arrows. Some of them were near misses but most of them were nowhere near the mark. After each shot he tried to retrieve the arrow but sometimes they were lost for good; at last he only had two left. Frans threw his spear at a rabbit that sought refuge inside a tree. He didn't have any more luck than his younger brother but at least the spear was easier to recover.

Although they didn't have much success, they had lots of fun. After every shot Dirk boasted how close he had come. As a hunter, he felt he was a big success.

Suddenly they heard a rifle shot in the distance, and shortly afterward, a second one. Dirk was suddenly alert. "Shall we go see who's hunting?"

Frans hesitated. "It's either a German or a member of the N.S.B.," he replied. "Nobody else has firearms." But his curiosity had been aroused too. And when Dirk persisted, Frans gave in. They ran off in the direction of the shots.

They crossed a potato field, jumped over a ditch, crossed a pasture, squirmed under some barbed wire and then made their way through a small wood lot. On the other side of the wood lot was a bicycle trail. Just as they were about to cross it, Frans saw two cyclists approaching, each with a rifle slung over his shoulder. He quickly dropped to the ground among the bushes and pulled Dirk down beside him.

As usual, Dirk had seen nothing. "Let go of me!" he snapped huffily.

"Hush, they're coming."

From Frans's tone of voice Dirk knew that he wasn't kidding, so he stopped struggling. "Who?" he whispered.

"Two men armed with rifles. I'd sooner they didn't see us."

The boys edged back until they were completely hidden by the bushes. But there wasn't much foliage left on the bushes, so their cover was pretty thin. Frans hoped that the cyclists hadn't seen them. The men had come around the bend just as the boys had been about to cross the path.

The cyclists rode in single file. The second one was talking, rather loudly, to make himself heard. They were almost even with the boys, who were lying flat on the ground. Frans lifted his head a moment to see who they were.

Just as he had thought: they were members of the new police force, the National Guard, but he didn't recognize either one of them. The one in the lead had a dead rabbit hanging from his handlebars. Frans caught a snatch of their conversation: " . . . but our friend Dreumel isn't going to forget about it, you can count on that. And that cripple has a lot more to answer for. For starters, Dreumel wants to scale the brick wall behind his house and then poke around to see . . ."

The rest was unintelligible. The cyclists disappeared around a bend in the path. The boys decided to wait for a minute, in case they came back.

"Did you see that?" blurted Dirk. "That sure was a fat

rabbit! Too bad it's going to end up in the wrong stomachs. That's the one we should have had. Boy, would Mother have been surprised!"

Frans nodded, but his thoughts were elsewhere. He repeated the snatch of conversation he had overheard to himself. What did it mean? He couldn't figure it out. He knew who Dreumel was, but the rest wasn't at all clear.

A flock of ducks rose up from the swamps near the pasture. They swooped low passing right over the place where the boys were hiding. Dirk reached for his bow and fired off his last two arrows.

He missed them by a city block. The ducks continued in the same direction the two cyclists had gone. Frans and Dirk watched them go and a few seconds later two shots rang out. Two ducks fell from the sky.

"Those Nazis again!" Dirk stamped his foot angrily, but a second later he had forgotten his resentment. "Did you see that one arrow, Frans? Boy, that was close! Next time I'll—"

"You've got no arrows left," Frans remarked drily.

Dirk realized Frans was right. His last two arrows had ended up somewhere in the underbrush, lost for good.

When he saw the disappointment on Dirk's face, Frans felt sorry for him. "Next week we'll make some new ones," he consoled him. "But now we better go home, otherwise we'll be late for supper. We always eat early on Saturday."

Being late for supper was one of the worst things Dirk could imagine. So he went willingly, and he was soon playing the hero again.

Darkness was setting in. Fog began to collect here and there in the meadows. The boys arrived home just as Mother was setting the table. They had just enough time to wash their hands.

For the first few minutes Dirk didn't say a word; he was too busy eating. But after supper he described their hunting adventure and all the rabbits, ducks, pheasants, and partridges he had almost shot. He had a spellbound, indulgent audience.

Frans then added the story about the conversation he had overheard. His father was dumbfounded. He asked Frans to repeat word for word what he had heard.

"Do you know what it means, Dad?" Frans asked.

"No . . . yes . . . Well, maybe . . ." he mumbled evasively. He wasn't about to commit himself further, but he was silent and preoccupied the rest of the evening.

CHAPTER III

Tarred and Feathered

Next Wednesday afternoon Frans and Dirk went back to Van Beveren. Their father had already paid him several visits. He told them that he had been glad to see his old mate, but for the rest he didn't say much about the visits. When the boys insisted he tell them more, their father told them a few funny stories about the time he and Janus had served in the army.

On Monday morning Father and Dries had taken a wagonload of wood to Van Beveren. The boys had ridden along as far as the school. They hadn't been able to see whether anything else was in the wagon, and Father had said very little about the delivery and the Monday morning visit.

But today they got their chance. Before they left home that morning, Father had told them to stop at Van Beveren's after school to pick up a letter. He told Frans to put the letter in his inside pocket and then to come straight home. They were warned not to make any detours or get into trouble. "And remember," Father told him, "don't discuss this with anyone!"

The boys made a solemn promise. There were so many things you couldn't talk about freely these days. They didn't ask any further questions either, they knew Dad didn't like questions. It made the visit to Van Beveren mysterious and exciting. They felt like genuine members of the Resistance.

They were very careful not to run into Dreumel. They hadn't seen him since that first day, but they might easily run into him somewhere. They hoped that the Nazi sympathizer would no longer recognize them, but they couldn't bank on that. So they looked around very carefully before they turned down each street.

Their enemy, however, was nowhere to be seen. They reached Van Beveren's house without any incident. You could see that once the house had been very posh, but that had been a long time ago. Now the door was almost bare of paint.

Frans yanked the doorbell. It took quite a while before the door was opened. He was just about to ring the bell again when Van Beveren's face appeared in one of the windows. Beaming, the old man opened the door, then closed it right away and secured the safety lock. "Come on in, boys. Glad to see you again."

"We've come to pick up a letter for Dad, sir," said Frans.

"Don't sir me, young man. I've told you that before! Just call me Uncle Janus, that sounds much better. Forget that letter for a minute; let's go see my wife first."

Van Beveren opened one of the doors in the long corridor and ushered them inside. His wife was sitting by a potbellied stove, sewing. "Meet Frans and Dirk Mulders. This is my wife," explained Uncle Janus.

The boys were no longer bashful in the man's presence. His wife was a very pleasant, kind lady with graying hair. She was much smaller than her husband. She put her sewing aside, pulled two chairs up to the stove and asked the boys if they wanted a cup of tea.

Before they could answer, Uncle Janus said, "Never mind that stuff; I've got a couple of nice apples for you. They're much better for you."

Frans and Dirk didn't argue; they were much too fond of apples, especially now that they were scarce. He gave each of them two, one for now and one for the road. They hardly dared accept this generous gift, because apples were terribly expensive, but Van Beveren only laughed. "Fuel is expensive too. We ran out of coal long ago and our wood was getting low too. But your dad took care of that." He pointed to a crate full of wood standing behind the potbellied stove.

The boys felt right at home with these two generous, warm-hearted people. As usual, Dirk did most of the talking. "We were worried that we might run into that Dreumel," he explained.

"Dreumel? I wouldn't worry about him! I'm sure he's still trying to scrub himself clean!" Uncle Janus and his wife burst out laughing so hard that Frans and Dirk looked at each other dumbfounded. "Scrubbed clean," what did he mean? They didn't understand it at all.

Uncle Janus looked at their faces and burst out laughing again. "I'll tell you the whole story. It's the funniest thing we've seen in a long time." He leaned back in his chair and began his story.

"You know there's a wall out back with a door that leads to the alley. Almost all the paint has blistered off that door and I wanted to give it a new coat, but paint is almost impossible to get.

"Well, I did have a drum of tar, from before the war. Tar may not look as nice as paint, but it's good for wood. So I thought, why don't I tar the door? Monday afternoon I rolled the drum to the door and loosened the lid. I wanted to do the outside of the door first so I took a stepladder into the alley, because the door is pretty high and I didn't want to get covered with tar. But I left the drum in the yard right behind the door.

"I was just about to take a pailful of tar out of the drum when my wife came out to tell me we had customers. She said she couldn't manage alone. You probably know I sell potatoes and vegetables. There isn't all that much; the Jerries are afraid that the people might get too fat and that wouldn't be healthy.

"At any rate, there was no end to the customers. So I closed the door to the alley and locked it. I usually do that. I replaced the lid on the barrel of tar, but I left the stepladder in the alley. That was a bit careless perhaps, but I thought I'd be right back.

"But it didn't turn out that way. After the customers had left some men showed up who had some business to discuss. In the meantime it got quite dark. When the men left, supper was ready. Afterwards I helped my wife with the dishes, that's one of my less exciting hobbies.

"Anyway, we got the dishes done and I was just about to sit down with my pipe when we heard a loud crash and a horrible scream outside. It came from the backyard and I jumped right up to see what had happened.

"I took the coal oil lamp out with me. You're not supposed to take a light outside with you, but this was an emergency; it sounded like somebody was in bad trouble. I couldn't begin to describe the yammering and screaming that went on! My wife had heard the noise too. She accompanied me outside.

"Well, we didn't have far to look. The cursing and wailing led us right to the tar barrel. As we approached, a black, ghastly looking specter rose out of the barrel. Somebody had fallen in. The only part of his body that wasn't covered with tar was his face, and when I shone the light on it, I recognized it immediately: it was Dreumel!

"What a shame, I thought. The guy had spoiled a drum of good tar. It dripped from all his clothes. Naturally I couldn't help him; otherwise I'd have gotten tar all over myself. Besides, Dreumel is a member of the N.S.B. and they wear black uniforms anyway. I wasn't about to ruin a good set of clothes. He didn't appreciate my help anyway, even though I

took great pains to throw some light on the subject."

Uncle Janus told his story with the dry humor that was his trademark but the sparkle in his eyes betrayed his satisfaction. Frans and Dirk burst out laughing. In fact, Dirk laughed so hard, he fell off his chair.

"Take it easy, Dirk, it gets worse," warned Van Beveren with a look of mock gravity on his face. "Accidents usually happen in bunches, at least, so Dreumel discovered."

"Right beside the drum was a large crate. You see, I grow tulips along the inside of the wall to give us a little color come spring. I used to cover the tulip beds with peat, but that stuff is so scarce now you can no longer get it. Fortunately, your dad provided me with a crateful of sawdust which I intended to use for the tulip beds. That crate arrived last Monday with the firewood. I put it outside, right next to the drum of tar because I wanted to cover the beds right after I finished painting the door. There was a cover on the crate but it wasn't on very tight.

"Anyway, Dreumel had trouble getting out of the barrel. He saw the crate standing right next to it and decided to climb on it. Crack, went the lid, and the poor sap broke right through it and tumbled right into my beautiful sawdust!"

Uncle Janus halted for a moment to give the boys a chance to pull themselves together. They were both hysterical.

"I won't try to describe what he looked like when he rose from the crate of sawdust. There are just no words for it. But I thought to myself: I've got to get him out of here, before any more accidents happen. So I moved the barrel of tar aside and quickly opened the door to the alley.

"I didn't have to tell him to get out. He got the message and was gone like a shot. Come to think of it, he didn't even say goodbye. He was out in the alley and around the corner in a flash.

"Just to be on the safe side, I moved the stepladder into the yard and locked the door again. Now you know why I said he probably hasn't even finished cleaning himself!"

The boys understood all right. Only, they were still unable to speak. It took a few minutes for them to catch their breath and then Dirk asked, "What did he want anyway?"

Uncle Janus shrugged his shoulders. "He didn't get around to telling me. But I have a pretty good idea. Sometimes these Nazis get pretty nosy. He probably thought there were things going on in my house that his friends, the Germans, should know about. You can't tell much from the front of the house, so he probably thought he would try the back.

"I always lock the door in the brick wall, so he had to climb over it. Since the stepladder was still in the alley, he had no trouble climbing across. But even then it's tricky to get across the wall because of the broken glass cemented in the top. But lucky for him just above the door most of the glass was broken off, so that's where he climbed over. Luck was really with him, for then he saw the barrel standing beside the door. And there was a lid on it. It couldn't have been better. So he lowered himself onto the lid. Only the lid hadn't been fastened properly and it flipped. Suddenly there he was, right up to his neck in tar."

"Have you heard from him since?" asked Frans, barely able to control his fits of laughter.

"No, not yet. Of course, I could lay charges against him. He was trespassing and, besides, he carried off at least ten liters of my precious tar and quite a bit of the sawdust . . . But, ah well, I'm a man of compassion, so I'll let it go this time. There was enough tar left to do the door and the shed. A lot of the sawdust had been spoiled, of course, but when I skimmed that off, enough was left to cover the tulip beds. Well boys, I don't think you should tell this story all over town, but you have my permission to amuse the folks back home with it. And now I'll give you that letter, Frans."

Uncle Janus got up and walked to a small china cabinet from which he removed a large, yellow envelope. Frans took it and shoved it in the inside pocket of his coat. The boys then said goodbye to their friendly host. They thanked him for the apples and promised to come again soon.

Van Beveren showed them out. "Now you boys go straight home, and no monkey business, promise?"

Back outside, they felt pretty important. "We're like two couriers who have to deliver a secret message," Dirk fantasized out loud.

"Shut up, you dunce!" snapped Frans, quickly glancing about to see if anyone had heard. About ten meters away an elderly lady bent over her walking stick, but she didn't pay any attention to the boys. A German staff car suddenly rounded the street corner. The boys stood as if nailed to the ground, but the car roared past and nothing happened.

They walked a little faster; in the city it was never altogether safe. Not until they had reached the Kanaaldijk, and the safety of open fields and water, did they relax a little.

Dirk hadn't said anything for quite a while; he was still

ashamed that he hadn't been able to keep his mouth shut. But since there had been no unpleasant consequences his good cheer and exuberance soon returned. "Boy, Uncle Janus is quite a guy! I don't think I've ever laughed so hard in my life."

"Uncle Janus pulled that off very nicely," remarked Frans.

"You're right . . . Pulled it off? What do you mean? He didn't know about it ahead of time, did he?"

"Well, that's what he pretended, and that was probably the wisest thing to do. He had to make it look like it was just a coincidence. At first I didn't see through it either, but then I was suddenly reminded of those two policemen we overheard. They were talking about a cripple, remember? Well, Uncle Janus has a game leg, and that's what those two guys were talking about. They said that Dreumel planned to climb the fence to have a look-see in the backyard. That's what the one guy said. I didn't connect it with Van Beveren's backyard at first, because there's a wall there, not a fence. Of course, that policeman didn't know that. But I told Dad all about it and he must have made the connection. Dad must have told Van Beveren Monday morning, and Van Beveren set up the rest."

Dirk's eyes bulged with astonishment. "Of course! That's how it went!"

"I believe so anyway. But we mustn't let on that we know! Uncle Janus thinks it's safer to have everybody think it was just a coincidence, so we better go along with it," Frans said emphatically.

Dirk promised to play his part. Secretly, he admired his older brother, who often showed a good deal more sense than he did.

CHAPTER IV

Midnight Discovery

Dad was waiting for them when they got home. "You're late," he said. "Did you get the letter, Frans?"

"Yes, Dad." Frans took out the letter. He hoped that Father would open it and show them what it said. But he stuffed the envelope into his pocket and went back to the mill.

During supper, Frans and Dirk told the story of Dreumel's encounter with the barrel of tar and the box of sawdust. The kitchen echoed with glee and laughter. Dries was especially tickled by the whole incident.

When they had settled down, Father said, "It's a very funny story and probably exactly what that Nazi deserved, but don't let the story get around. Dreumel already has a grudge against you and also against Van Beveren. If this story gets around and he becomes a laughing stock, there's no telling what he might do."

"Do you think he's a German spy, Dad?" Dirk asked.

His father nodded. "I think so. Uncle Janus will have to keep an eye on him. Dreumel will try to avenge himself and, don't forget, he's got the Germans behind him. It may all look very funny today, but it's a question of who will have the last laugh. I wish Janus had been a little more careful. Sometimes he goes too far."

"But this wasn't his fault. It all happened by accident," Frans remarked drily.

A hint of a smile came to Father's face. "Well, let's assume so. In any case, you're not to breathe a word of this to anyone. And another thing: I plan to use you as couriers more often. But then you'll have to remember three things: keep your eyes open, keep your ears open, and forget what you've seen and heard. Understood? It's a lesson you'd better learn very quickly, because your own lives as well as those of others might depend on it. Always remember that!"

Father was dead serious. Both boys nodded silently.

Couriers. That was the word Dirk had used earlier that afternoon. Then it was only a dream, now it was a reality. Life had suddenly become very exciting. But it was no game.

After supper Frans and Dirk were allowed to stay up for another hour. Then they were sent upstairs to their bedroom. Each had his own bed. After they had said their evening prayers and Mother had tucked them in, she went back downstairs.

The boys weren't sleepy at all. They continued to talk in low voices about the day's experiences. Dirk, of course, did most of the talking, but after half an hour he fell silent. His regular, deep breathing told Frans that he had fallen asleep.

Frans lay awake for a long time, but finally he dropped off too. Suddenly he was awakened by a dull roar overhead that was rapidly growing louder. He was still groggy, but he immediately knew what it was—Allied planes! They flew over almost every night on their way to Germany.

The dull, steady roar was suddenly interspersed with anti-aircraft fire. The anti-aircraft installations were on the other side of the city.

Frans had to have a look. He wanted to know what had happened to the airplanes. Suppose one of them was hit!

He checked to see if Dirk was also awake, but, no, he was still fast asleep. Mother often said, "During the day he's a real livewire, but at night an explosion wouldn't even wake him." Frans laughed softly. Mother was right: not even the ear-splitting racket outside was enough to wake Dirk.

Frans quietly slipped out of the bed and walked to the window. The windows were covered with heavy drapes as no light was allowed to show outside. But now Frans drew the curtain aside a little; there was no light in the bedroom anyway.

It was much lighter outside than he had thought. There was a full moon and practically no clouds. The huge mill cast a black silhouette against the light night sky, and the silver light of the moon was reflected in the water of the canal.

The Allied bombers were somewhere directly overhead. Frans couldn't see them, but the roar told him where they were. The Germans kept up a steady barrage, but the planes were flying very high and the anti-aircraft batteries seemed to have no effect at all. As the bombing formation passed out of range, the guns fell silent.

For a while Frans remained at the window. In the light of the full moon the world looked enchanting, completely different than in the daytime. The noise of the bombers gradually died away. Frans was thinking about the men in the airplanes. On any given bombing mission they would be fired upon many times, but if they made it through the anti-aircraft fire, their job was to kill people with their terrible bombs.

War—what a horrible thing! Frans could get very upset at the Germans, those cruel oppressors. He was glad of the Allied bombing raids, of course; yet he felt very sorry for the people on whom those bombs would fall.

He shivered, it was getting cold. He decided he'd better get back to bed. He took one last glance at the surrounding countryside, letting his glance linger on the mill—the lone sentinel stationed high on the Kanaaldijk as if it were guarding the countryside behind it.

But what was that? Was there a light burning in the top of the mill? High in the top of the mill was a window covered with black cloth, but Frans thought he saw light behind it. That was strange! Surely Dad and Dries wouldn't be working there this time of night. But then why the light?

He was puzzled and also somewhat concerned. Suddenly something else caught his eye. Something was moving on the glistening water of the canal, a dark shape. It was a rowboat with five men crossing from the far side to the Kanaaldijk. Frans recognized the boat: it was theirs. Dad often used it instead of walking all the way back to the bridge.

The boat had reached the near shore. The first one to get out was Dries. Father wasn't among them. But who were the other men? Three of them he couldn't recognize, but the fourth man limped. That had to be Van Beveren!

The men followed Dries into the mill and the door closed behind them.

Wide awake now, Frans stayed to watch, but nothing else happened. Finally he crawled back into bed. But sleep was out of the question. He was sure he'd made an important discovery, and he tried to figure it all out.

Dries accompanied by four men, one of whom was Uncle Janus. Father had to be in the mill; Frans thought he'd seen a shadow pass across the window once or twice . . . But what were they doing in the middle of the night? Frans had a bit of an idea: it was a secret meeting of some sort. But why?

The Germans imposed a strict curfew. No person was allowed outside at night without a special permit. Uncle Janus and the other three men must have come from the city. They hadn't come along the Kanaaldijk, but had probably followed one of the many trails that led through the woods and across the fields. There was lots of cover there, and the risk of being detected was very small. Then Dries had rowed across the canal to fetch them.

Frans tried to reconstruct the scene. He was reminded of the letter Uncle Janus had given them. If he had only seen the letter; that probably explained the whole thing. Van Beveren was probably a member of the Resistance. They were people who carried out all kinds of "illegal" or underground activities against the Germans, trying to frustrate the German war effort in every way possible.

Were Dad and Dries also members of the Resistance? They had never said anything about it, but Frans often had the feeling that things were happening inside the mill that neither he nor Dirk had been told about. Now he had proof. He decided he wouldn't discuss it with anyone, however, especially not with Dirk.

Darn! If only he were a couple of years older! Then he could be part of the organization. He was much too young to help with the actual work, of course, but at least he could help by being a courier!

Frans lay there thinking for about an hour. Now and then he would raise his head and listen for sounds from the mill. But, no, he heard nothing. It was just his imagination. At long last his mind fogged. He fell asleep and dreamed about run-ins with the Germans, about raids, and spies and English flyers, and about doing many heroic and patriotic deeds.

When he awoke the next morning, he was only half rested. It took awhile before he realized that his heroic adventures had only been a dream. But he knew that he had really seen Dries and four other men in the boat. There was something secretive going on, and, who knows, he might eventually learn more about it.

During breakfast he eyed his father and Dries inquisitively, but their looks betrayed nothing. Dries yawned a couple of times, probably because he hadn't had enough sleep. But their talk told him nothing about the mysterious events of the past night.

After breakfast Frans and Dirk got ready for school. They put their coats on, shoved their meager lunches into their pockets and left. With the wind in their backs they made pretty good time. The brisk wind also blew the last cobwebs and fantasies from Frans's mind. He was almost beginning to think everything had been a dream, even the boat and the four men.

Dirk had taken along a ball and he kicked it down the road. The wind got under it and hurled it into the canal. Dirk was dismayed, but Frans knew what to do. He cut a willow branch and maneuvered the ball back to shore.

At the bridge they ran into a German sentry. There had never been a sentry there before. The boys tensed. Suppose the German knew about yesterday's letter . . . Heads down, they walked past the sentry, who paid no attention to them.

Five minutes later they reached the town square. A group of people had gathered in front of the police station. Many of them were grinning and chuckling softly. Just as the boys arrived, a German officer stormed out of the building. He looked upset, and when he saw the crowd in front of the building, he grew livid and screamed at them in German. The boys didn't understand what he was saying, but the message

was loud and clear—to everybody. The crowd scattered in all directions.

The boys spotted Mr. Lammerts, the fourth grade teacher. He had been in the crowd in front of the police station. Mr. Lammerts saw the boys too. He waited for the boys to catch up and then said, "It sure is windy today. That should make your father happy. Now at least he can operate the mill."

"That doesn't do much good if you haven't got any grain to mill. The Germans have taken everything," said Frans. He knew it was safe to speak his mind to Mr. Lammerts, for he had no use for the Germans either.

"That's true, but sometimes they drop a stitch here and there, as we've just seen," replied the teacher happily.

The boys looked at him questioningly. What did he mean?

Mr. Lammerts saw they didn't understand, so he told them what had happened. "Three prisoners escaped from the police station last night. They were members of the Resistance who had been arrested a few days ago. They were about to be turned over to the German S.D. for intensive questioning."

Mr. Lammerts halted a moment as a German staff car roared by. Now the boys knew what the fuss was all about. The S.D. was the German security police, which hunted down everyone who was anti-German. Many who had the misfortune of being interrogated by the S.D. did not survive.

"How did they escape?" asked Dirk.

The teacher shrugged his shoulders. "I don't know exactly, but some of the people said that the bars of the cell windows had been cut. The three Resistance men were all together in one cell. They apparently crawled through the window into the courtyard. But there's a wall around the courtyard with a single exit and that was securely locked. Yet the lock had been picked and the men had escaped. It would have been impossible without help from outside. The Germans are furious, of course. You can bet they'll do everything they can to recover their prisoners."

They had reached the school and Mr. Lammerts went inside. Frans and Dirk stayed outside in the schoolyard and joined some of the other kids. They were playing a game and Dirk quickly joined in. A few minutes later the bell rang and everyone filed inside.

A group of sixth graders was discussing the escape. They were speculating how the men had managed to get out and where they were hiding. Of course nobody knew for sure. Frans joined the group, but he was content to listen. His expression betrayed nothing, but in his mind's eye he once again saw the moonlit canal and the rowboat containing Dries, Uncle Janus and three unknown figures, who disappeared into the mill.

CHAPTER V

Fugitives

In the days that followed Frans's suspicions were confirmed. Three strangers were hiding in the mill. Their hiding place was high in the crown. During the day two of them often helped in the sawmill, while the third kept watch upstairs. Through the windows on either side of the mill he could keep the whole dike under surveillance. Whenever strangers came toward the mill, he pushed a button connected to a bell in the sawmill. Immediately the other two would scurry upstairs.

Frans knew very well who they were, but Dirk noticed nothing. Frans also realized that he couldn't discuss this with anyone, so he carefully kept his mouth shut. But Frans was anxious to find out more about the three fugitives. Occasionally he would hint at the subject, but the other members of the household told him nothing.

The Dutch and German police had been searching for the escapees for days, but to no avail. For some reason they hadn't bothered the Mulders. Without a direct search, no one would find out that the men were here.

Three weeks later they were gone. It came as quite a surprise to Frans. After supper that evening when he was alone with his father, he couldn't resist raising the subject. His father was sitting at his desk in the corner of the room doing the bookkeeping. Dirk had already gone upstairs to bed. Everyone had left the room except Frans. "Dad, are they gone? I mean the three men in the mill."

His father looked at him; his face was serious, yet calm. "Yes, Frans, they're gone."

"Where did they go, Dad? Were they the men who—" He stopped. His father had put down his pen and shook his finger at Frans. Instantly, Frans blushed, but his father wasn't angry, only dead serious.

"Listen, my boy. I know of a courageous man who did a lot of things for his country, for the church, and for others. But they were things the Germans had forbidden. He did them anyway because he couldn't do anything else. He believed that God wanted him to do them."

Father halted for a moment. Frans stared at the floor.

"One day, over a year ago, the Germans arrested him. They searched his house but found nothing incriminating. His wife went to the police station and asked the S.D. to release her husband. They just laughed at her. They knew everything her husband had done, and they told her how they knew. There was no sinister spying involved, no deliberate treason. The men of the S.D. and their Dutch friends had picked up the information simply by listening to people talk. These people didn't mean anything by it; they were simply people who knew something or perhaps only suspected something and who couldn't keep their mouths shut.

"The man himself never betrayed the cause, no matter how cruelly the Germans interrogated him. But all his courage and resolve didn't help him. The Germans sent him to a concentration camp, and he may now well be dead—indirectly killed by people who 'didn't mean anything by it,' but who simply wanted to know too much or tell more than they knew."

Frans felt very ill at ease; he knew exactly what his father was talking about. He made one last effort to defend himself.

"I'll never tell anybody, Dad."

A smile came to his father's face and the gravity disappeared. "I know that, Frans. I've never doubted it, because I know you very well. In fact, Dirk's doing remarkably well too. And he probably doesn't even understand what's going on.

"You mustn't think that I don't trust you, Frans. That's not the point. But the less you know, the less you're responsible for. So don't ask me to confirm what you suspect. If we all survive, one day I'll tell you everything."

Mother entered the room and said, "Frans, it's your bedtime! In fact, it's already way past your bedtime."

Obediently Frans got up. Fifteen minutes later he was in bed. But his father's words were deeply imprinted on his mind. It wasn't the first time he had discussed such things with his father, but the discussion had never been quite this serious. Frans resolved never to ask for information about things that might jeopardize the family or others, things that were forbidden by the Germans. His father and Dries were involved in things that could easily cost them their lives; he didn't want to be responsible for "indirectly killing" them.

That was his last thought of the day.

In the weeks that followed, other strangers visited the mill and sometimes stayed for long periods of time. Then one day they would be gone, and Frans and Dirk never knew where they had disappeared to.

Frans, of course, was much more aware of what was happening than Dirk. Since he had had his heart to heart chat with his father, Frans was sometimes allowed to help. This usually took the form of bringing food to the fugitives in the mill. He never asked any questions, but kept his eyes and ears open.

The boys' visits to Van Beveren also became more frequent. Sometimes it was just to drop off a letter, and sometimes just to see whether Uncle Janus had a message for their father. If so, Uncle Janus usually wrote the message on a piece of paper and sealed it in an envelope so that the boys wouldn't be able to read it. But Frans noticed that almost in-variably such a message would result in the appearance of a few more fugitives. He also had the impression that many of these people were Jews. Many of them, he learned, came from Amsterdam.

Although he never asked any questions, Frans turned these observations over in his mind and gradually the picture became clearer. Hitler and his henchmen were determined to exterminate all Jews. The Nazis claimed that there were good and bad races. The best, the most noble, was the Aryan race, to which all people of German ancestry belonged. That race would some day rule the world. The worst race, the most subhuman, they claimed, was the Jewish race. It had to be ex-terminated at all cost, because it was the source of all evil in the world.

Occasionally Father talked about these things when the family was together in the living room. Father also said that racism was godless, completely at odds with the Bible, and that God would certainly punish the Germans for what they were doing to the Jews.

Most Dutch Jews had already been transported to concen-tration camps in both Holland and Germany, only to be taken to extermination camps in Poland later. But many Jews had gone into hiding too. They were usually given another name and smuggled to secret hiding places throughout the country.

Before the war Amsterdam had hosted a huge Jewish population. In fact, Uncle Janus, who used to live in Amster-dam, came from a district that was almost exclusively Jewish. He must have gotten to know quite a few of them. And now he was involved in a secret organization that helped spirit away as many Jews as possible.

Frans thought that was very courageous. He also admired his parents and Dries who tried to help these victims of Nazi persecution. He could understand his parents and Dries being involved, but Van Beveren and his wife weren't even

Christians. In fact, they didn't even belong to a church. And yet they helped their neighbors, while, on the other hand, many church people never lifted a finger to help the Jews.

Frans had raised this question recently, but his father hadn't responded. That evening, however, he had read Luke 10 verses 25 to 37, the parable of the Good Samaritan who saw his duty more clearly than either the priest or the Levite. After reading the passage, his father had said, "You see a lot of that happening today. Through their deeds, non-Christians often put Christians to shame."

This and many other things gave Frans a lot to think about. But not Dirk, why should he worry? Sometimes he became aware that there were strangers in the mill, but he never questioned it, and he never suspected that Van Beveren might have something to do with it. He was satisfied just knowing that he and Frans were helping by being couriers. Actually, it was more of a game than a cause for him. The visits were always a pleasant change of pace. Van Beveren often gave them an apple or something. Better yet, he always had exciting stories to tell, mostly about years ago, but sometimes also about things that had happened recently. The boys were always spellbound. Sometimes they could hardly control their laughter, especially when Van Beveren told them about some of the pranks he had pulled while in the army.

Twice they ran into their archenemy, Dreumel. The first time Frans spotted him early enough for them to duck into a side street, but the second time it was too late. Their first inclination was to turn and run, but Frans realized just in time that that would certainly give them away. They quickly turned to look into a store window, their backs to the sidewalk. Dreumel paid no attention to them. That was all that had happened, but they had been shaken nevertheless. Still, it had given them hope that the Nazi sympathizer no longer remembered them. All in all, they decided they'd better try to stay out of his way.

CHAPTER VI

A Painful Decision

Almost a month had gone by and the war had carried into the dark days of December. The days were generally cold and foggy. Darkness came early, hastened by dense fog that blocked the thin, watery rays of the December sun. The fog was cold and damp and soaked through your clothes in less than half an hour.

The front door opened and Mr. Mulders and his son Dries came out. They closed the door softly behind them and were quickly swallowed up by the impenetrable darkness. Even the mill, which was right next to the house, was completely enshrouded. But that didn't bother the two men. They could find their way with their eyes closed. Without hesitation they walked up the narrow path to the mill door and then quietly slipped inside. There were no fugitives in the mill now. It was not a permanent refuge, only a halfway house for people enroute to permanent destinations. They might soon have visitors again, as soon as they got a message from Van Beveren, but for now the mill was vacant.

In fact, they had received a message from Van Beveren that afternoon, saying he wanted to talk with Mulders and Dries and a couple of other men. Mulders had no idea what his old army buddy wanted. The messages carried by Frans and Dirk were usually so cryptic that you couldn't make heads or tails out of them. If, for example, it said, "I can deliver three red cabbages," it meant that he wanted to send three fugitives that same day. If the message simply read, "cabbages," it meant the fugitives would come the next day. If a message ever fell into the wrong hands, nobody would be able to figure it out.

Yesterday's message read, "Can you deliver a bag of sawdust today? I need some for myself and for a couple of friends as well." Roughly, that meant: I need advice and will come tonight accompanied by a couple of others.

Mulders first wanted to keep Dries out of it, but the boy had seen the message and insisted on being part of it. Father decided maybe it was just as well. He knew that Dries was very capable and clever for his age. He was very proud of his son. Dries had already been in on some dangerous actions, and he knew how to keep his mouth shut.

Mulders knew that Van Beveren was up to his ears in the Resistance. He helped Jews and passed along many other fugitives. He had contacts with people who prepared false identity cards, and he did many other things Mulders didn't know much about and, to be honest, didn't want to know about.

Janus was just as he remembered him: very capable and very courageous. Mulders admired him but secretly wondered whether some of the things he did weren't a mite too chancy. Would Van Beveren finally hang himself, as so many before him had?

But Mulders himself was involved too. There was nothing else he could do. When there was need, when innocent people were persecuted and even killed, something had to be done.

Mr. Mulders and his son waited downstairs in the mill. Van Beveren and his associates usually didn't take the Kanaaldijk, but cut through the woods and the fields. When they reached the other side of the canal, Van Beveren usually hooted like an owl. That was the signal for Mulders or Dries to take the rowboat to the other side to pick them up.

They listened anxiously but the minutes ticked by and all remained quiet. Mr. Mulders was becoming uneasy. They were late. Had something gone wrong? Then he remembered that it was very foggy. It would be very difficult for them to find their way.

Father and son talked quietly if only to suppress their growing concern. Then there was a sudden knock on the door. They were instantly alert, and Mulders stealthily tiptoed to the door. Then he heard Janus's voice: "Open up, we're friends!"

Relieved, Mulders unlocked the door. It was Van Beveren all right, accompanied by two other men, young men who had been here before. "We came down the Kanaaldijk," explained Uncle Janus laughingly. "There's no danger now, because you can't see a thing and all the Jerries are huddled around the home fires. We got here later than I had planned, because it's so foggy it's hard to see where you're going. At any rate, we're here."

Mulders carefully locked the door again. Then he escorted his friends upstairs, to the upper story. He made sure the curtains were closed before lighting the coal oil lamp. There was hardly enough room for the five men. There were only two chairs, but one of the men sat on a crate and two others on a cot. It didn't matter. The important thing was that they had made it.

Van Beveren immediately got down to business. "We've got problems," he said. "We're getting more and more fugitives. These people all have to be sheltered. We can take care of that aspect. But we need counterfeit identity papers, ration cards, travel permits, etc. Fugitives staying on farms could probably survive without ration cards, but for those in the cities, it's impossible."

Van Beveren halted. Mulders wondered what his old friend was driving at.

"There's only one way to fill the need: we have to steal ration cards and other papers from local distribution centers. That's been going on for some time already, but we just got word from upstairs that we have to intensify our raids if we're going to make the system work.

"It's not without danger. Anyone caught in a raid on a distribution center will be executed on the spot. But it has to be done. So we have to form a squad, right here, that can act on a moment's notice whenever it gets a chance.

"Now, you've helped us an awful lot, Koos, and I wanted to ask you if we can hide the stuff here. It's mostly a question of ration cards and identity cards, but if we can pick up weapons on the side, we'll do that too. We need them."

Van Beveren halted, but Mulders did not immediately reply. It presented a problem of conscience. Hiding Jews and other fugitives was one thing. Then you were talking about people who needed help. But what about this? Raids, robberies . . . and then hide the stolen goods here? Was that really necessary?

Uncle Janus understood Mulders' hesitation. "If I were to

ask you this in peacetime, you'd throw me out, and rightly so.
But this is war. You've got to realize what's at stake. These
Germans are hunting human beings. I used to live in Amsterdam—right in the middle of the Jewish quarter. I know hundreds of people who have been carried off by the Germans.
They were treated like animals, sent to concentration camps
and finally to extermination camps in Poland. Do you think
any of them will ever return? They're all going to be killed, I
tell you!

"That's what brought me into the Resistance. Janus Van
Beveren isn't about to stand around watching the Nazis butch-
er men, women, and children. And I know you feel the
same way. You've got your Christian convictions—that's why
you've helped us. But we can't stop here. The people we hide
need food and clothing and new identity cards, otherwise all
our other work is in vain too. We've got to build up a total
system. That's not flouting the law. You know that. The
Germans are flouting the law by what they are doing to our
country—plundering and pillaging it, persecuting our people,
and brutally exterminating innocent people."

Mulders didn't need to be convinced, really. He had known
this for quite some time. But he had trouble accepting it.
"You're right, Janus. Of course I'll go along, that is, if you
can use me in the raids."

But Janus smiled and shook his head. "That's not
necessary, my friend. I only want you to let us use your mill,
your house and your lumber to hide the stuff we bring in.
You're ideally situated here and I'm sure you can think up a
few good hiding places.

"And as for taking part in the raids, you're getting a bit too
old. That's for young, strong men. As a rule, I won't be directly involved either. My game leg would trip me up for sure. I'll
be able to give leadership because I've got lots of sources of
information. The orders will usually come from me, but Arie
and Egbert here will carry them out." Janus pointed to the

two young men with him. Arie was the one with the sturdy frame. He had friendly, brown eyes and brownish hair. He must have been twenty-five or so. Egbert looked younger, but he was a few inches taller and much leaner. His hair was very blond, almost white, and his eyes were bluish gray. Van Beveren gave only their first names, and even those were probably not their real ones.

"I'm glad you'll help us," continued Van Beveren. "To be honest, I had counted on it. Now we only have to recruit a couple more capable young men. I don't want any adventurers, but people committed to the cause. I've got my eye on a couple, but maybe you can help me out there too."

As if by coincidence, Janus's glance strayed to Dries, who had said nothing until now. But now he jumped up. "I'll help! Is it all right, Father?"

Aghast, Mulders shook his head vehemently. "Absolutely not! You're only seventeen."

"I'm almost eighteen, and I've already done a lot of dangerous things," replied Dries indignantly.

"Ah, I thought Dries was older," confessed Janus. "He's big and smart for his age, I see. As far as I'm concerned, he can join the squad, but he's your son, Koos, and I'll stick by your judgment. It is dangerous, I've told you that, and it's true. We won't do anything without your approval."

Dries looked downcast. He had fervently hoped that his father would give his permission. He knew that the work was dangerous, but he was prepared to sacrifice his life for his country and for those who needed help.

Van Beveren went on about something else, but neither Mr. Mulders nor his son could keep his mind on what he was saying. Anyway, the most important business had been settled.

Half an hour later the three visitors said goodbye. If they hurried, they could still make it back before curfew. No one was allowed out after curfew unless they had a special permit from the Germans.

Dries and his father only had a few meters to go. Dries was about to start talking about the squad again but his father interrupted him. "Go to bed, son. It can wait until tomorrow."

Disappointed and irritated, Dries obeyed. Why wasn't he allowed to join, he wondered. Why should it always be up to others? There were tens of thousands of English and American boys only a few months older than he, who were in the army. What difference did a few months make? But feeling sorry for himself didn't help; it only made matters worse. It took a long time before he fell asleep that night.

But it took his father even longer to get to sleep. Mrs. Mulders had stayed up to wait for him. She had been sewing and mending clothes all evening. Now she listened to her husband's account of the meeting. The two had no secrets from one another. Mulders told his wife everything Janus had said and what he had replied.

In the end they came to an agreement. To provide refuge for the unfortunates being hunted by the German police—that was one thing. To hide contraband stolen by the Resistance—that was all right too. But to involve Dries in the active work of the Resistance—no, that was too much.

It was quite late before they went to bed. They had come to an agreement, and yet . . .

Every night Mulders faithfully read a chapter from the Bible before going to sleep. Then he said his evening prayers, remembering the needs of the family, the church, the country and the queen residing in England. He always asked the Lord to deliver them from the evils of the German occupation and to bless all efforts toward that end.

His evening prayers always tended to be the same, because the needs were the same. Prayer usually gave him a measure of comfort and courage, but that evening it left him feeling restless and depressed.

He lay in bed beside his wife, but sleep just wouldn't come. He was tortured by doubts and agonized over his decisions. It had been three-and-a-half years ago that the Germans had unexpectedly pounced on his country. When, after five days of intensive fighting, the government had surrendered, many of the people had thought that the worst was over. But they had been sadly mistaken. Things had gone from bad to worse. Slowly they had been deprived of all their freedoms. Newspapers and radios only published German propaganda.

Clergymen who prayed for the queen or warned against the evils of National Socialism sooner or later ended up in concentration camps. All political parties had been disbanded, except, of course, the N.S.B. Christian schools were increasingly feeling the pressures of Nazification. All Jews were being picked up and transported. The country had been plundered and pillaged. Sometimes it seemed as though God didn't hear their prayers, prayers that rose to heaven by the hundreds of thousands.

Mulders knew better, of course. He knew that God always hears prayer. One day they would be liberated, but in the meantime how much suffering would they have to endure?

Sleep finally came, if it could be called sleep.

The next day there were many animated discussions between Mr. Mulders and his eldest son. They were together in the woodshed and for once they had no audience.

At first, Dries was aloof and moody. He was still stewing about his father's refusal to let him go. "Why shouldn't I be able to fight for my country?" he demanded.

His father met the question head on. He was very patient and listened attentively to what his son said, and then he gave him a calm answer. His patience and love won out; in the end, the matter was resolved and father and son were reconciled. Dries learned how hard it was for his father to face the possible consequences. His father would much rather expose himself to danger than to see his son gunned down at the age of seventeen!

But Mulders learned a few things too. He asked Dries

straight out why he wanted to join the squad. He found out that although Dries had difficulty putting his feelings into words, it wasn't simply a question of adventure. It was much deeper. Dries wanted to fight for the oppressed and persecuted against the demonic machine that did the oppressing and persecuting. And now there was an opportunity . . .

His mother was anxious, so she came to the shed to bring the men a cup of imitation coffee and to take part in the discussion. She stayed for almost an hour. When she left, there were tears in her eyes, which she quickly wiped away because she didn't want Nel to know what was going on.

That afternoon Dries harnassed the wagon and loaded some firewood, and a few other combustibles to bring to Van Beveren. Then father and son climbed aboard. Mr. Mulders didn't visit Van Beveren very often. It was better that people didn't know there was a connection between them. But this time he had to chance it.

They stayed away for a long time. When they returned, there was a satisfied glow on Dries's face. Mulders, on the other hand, looked grave, but not downcast or somber. The decision had been made, and he could live with it.

Van Beveren hadn't been surprised at all. He simply said, "I knew you'd come. I never doubted it for a moment. In fact, I had already made a mental note to put Dries on the list . . ."

And Mulders had to admit to himself that deep down inside he had also known that it would turn out this way.

CHAPTER VII

A Friend in Need

Christmas vacation was here. Frans and Dirk were exuberant: two glorious weeks without school! Nothing to do but fool around all day, play fight and go out on adventures. And there was always something to do around a mill.

Best of all, they had a friend to play with. He had come a few days ago—a Jewish fugitive from Amsterdam. His name was Jaap Roseboom and he was only a few months younger than Frans.

He had been brought one dark evening by Uncle Janus. Jaap was an orphan who had been raised by his uncle and aunt. But his uncle and aunt had been taken away by the Germans and would probably never return. Before reporting to the Germans as ordered, they had brought Jaap to friends. But he hadn't been able to stay there very long. The entire Jewish quarter in Amsterdam had been scoured for any remaining fugitives.

The boy had been sent from one address to another, staying just ahead of the Germans. That is, until he had ended up with Uncle Janus, who had known his parents when he lived in Amsterdam. Uncle Janus had promised to find him a good home, on a farm if possible. But it had taken longer than he had thought, and it might take even longer. So, for the time being Jaap had to stay with the Mulders.

Frans and Dirk didn't mind at all. Their minds swam with eager plans for the Christmas holidays. Young Jaap was very likeable. The first few days he had been quiet and withdrawn, as though he were afraid, but then he had good reason to be. He had been hunted like a wild animal for so long, he was naturally withdrawn.

But gradually he relaxed. He felt secure in the mill. Having a couple of boys his age to play with helped too. The three boys had a good time together. There were all kinds of things to do in the lumber shed: they could build all kinds of things from leftover lumber and could roll around in the sawdust to their hearts' content.

Frans and Dirk realized that no one was to know about Jaap's presence. And if anyone showed up at the mill, the boy had to vanish instantly. But in late December, when the days were short, there weren't very many callers at the old mill.

Mr. Mulders told the boys to be very careful, but they thought he was being overly cautious. What danger could there possibly be here? Gradually, Mr. Mulders himself became less jumpy. Eventually, Jaap ate with them at the family table. This was a new experience for the young fugitive. For months he had been locked up all alone in a tiny room in the city and now he was suddenly accepted into the family like one of the kids.

The prayers and Bible-reading at the dinner table were something entirely new to him. At first he looked somewhat surprised but made no comment.

Several days later, Mr. Mulders gave the boys permission to roam about in the fields and woods. Jaap said he would like nothing better. It gave him a feeling of freedom, something he hadn't felt for a very long time.

One day between Christmas and New Year the three again went out together. They were given the usual warnings: be careful and pay attention, avoid people, don't do anything foolish. That was easy enough to promise. They listened with only one ear to the list of cautions. Their eyes sparkled in anticipation. Frans and Dirk saw how excited and eager their new friend was. This also made them excited. Mother gave them each an apple for the road. Snip, the dog, went along too.

It had snowed a little the day before, and because it was just below freezing, the snow had not melted as it usually did. The conditions were ideal for following animal tracks. Not only could they easily track the animals, they'd be able to spot them very easily against the white background.

Frans was a skilful tracker. His father had taught him, for example, to distinguish between rabbit tracks and those made by hares. He could recognize fox tracks and even those of field mice, weasels and several kinds of birds. Dirk caught on pretty quickly. The two brothers tried to teach Jaap, but he could hardly believe that two young boys could be so knowledgeable about the great outdoors. To him, an inner city boy, it seemed like magic.

Snip was an excellent tracking dog, but of course he didn't use his eyes but his nose to follow the tracks.

Carefree and happy, they roamed through the fields. Whenever they came to a ditch they easily found a way across, or whenever they ran into barbed wire fences, they slid underneath. The boys knew that the farmers didn't mind. Everyone around here knew them. They were always wandering about the fields but were careful not to destroy anything. Besides, the harvest had long since been taken in.

Jaap had trouble keeping up with his new friends. He wasn't as strong and agile as they were because he had been cooped up so long. Especially when it came to jumping ditches, he sometimes had trouble. But he had no accidents, and he seemed to enjoy it. His cheeks, which had been colorless for months, glowed with excitement and the crisp outdoor air. Clearly, he was having a good time, probably the best he had had in years.

Frans and Dirk noticed Jaap's delight. They felt like heroes because they were helping someone directly. As usual Dirk was the most talkative of the three. He carried on as if he was an expert backwoodsman and knew all the hidden secrets of nature. Jaap was all ears. He made a real effort to remember everything the boys told him, but it was just too much.

A December day is short, but this one seemed longer, probably because of the snow.

Snip ran up and down the trails. Once he started barking excitedly when he found the entrance to a burrow. Another time, a crow, which he hadn't seen, swooped down in front of him, screeching and scolding. Snip was delighted. He barked furiously and insisted on having the last word as the angry bird winged off, leaving the field to the meddling foursome.

Then the dog picked up a trail that made him forget everything else. Holding his nose close to the ground, he waddled off across the snow. The boys couldn't pick up the scent, but they did see the tracks. Dirk claimed that they had been made by a cat, but Frans shook his head. "That's not a cat, no way. A cat leaves different prints and they're spaced differently. I think it's either a weasel or a skunk."

This was becoming exciting. Dirk thought they would catch up to the animal any moment. But he couldn't keep quiet, so Frans told him to keep his mouth shut, otherwise the animal would hear them coming and would be long gone by the time they got there. Frans was right, Dirk decided, so he kept silent. As quietly as possible they crunched on through the snow behind Snip.

Snip had stopped barking too; he was too busy trying to keep up with his prey. The boys had trouble keeping up with him. The tracks crisscrossed the field, leading first to the left, then to the right, then they made a large detour and soon the boys were back where they had started. They had to jump a couple of ditches, worm their way under barbed wire, and fight their way through thick underbrush.

Frans was becoming worried about the time. Shouldn't they be going back? It was already getting dark. But the excitement of the hunt was too big a temptation; they couldn't stop now. Neither Dirk nor Jaap had any idea of the time. Jaap even seemed to have forgotten that he was a Jewish fugitive and that he had to stay out of sight. He had become a different person.

The zig-zagging tracks led them further and further afield. Looking back, Frans couldn't even see the mill anymore. Again he was nagged by doubt. He was the oldest and should make the decisions. Just a few more minutes, and then . . .

Snip dove into a dry ditch and followed the trail along the dry bed. The boys followed the dog along the bank. The ditch ran straight toward a small country road. There it ended in a culvert that ran under the road. Snip halted at the entrance to the culvert. All of a sudden he seemed to have second thoughts. That was strange. The diameter of the culvert was at least half a meter and Snip wasn't very big. He could easily go in.

"Go on Snip!" urged Dirk.

The terrier danced around excitedly. He growled and whined, stuck his head into the culvert and then pulled it back again.

"He's scared to go into the culvert," suggested Jaap.

"He doesn't have to," replied Frans. He got down into the ditch, grabbed the dog's collar and pulled the dog, now loudly objecting, across the street to the other end of the culvert. But Snip refused to go on; he just stood at the other end of the culvert and growled menacingly.

Frans realized that the trail ended at the culvert. There were no tracks in the snow at this end. Apparently their prey was hiding in the culvert. He decided it would be better if Snip did not go inside after it. After all, he didn't know what it was, so

why take chances? Frans stooped to seize the dog's collar, but
he was too late. Suddenly overcoming his reluctance, Snip
slipped into the culvert.

Tensely, the boys waited. Several seconds went by and
nothing happened. Then they heard a strange hissing noise.
Frans bent down to look inside the culvert, but it was so dark
that he couldn't see a thing. Suddenly Snip began whining
piteously. The boys looked at one another in despair. If only
they could help! Frans now regretted that he hadn't called a
halt to the chase earlier.

The next moment the dog came charging out of the culvert,
still whining and sneezing. He shook his head wildly and
carried on as if he had gone berserk. A horrible stench floated
up from the concrete culvert. The boys pinched their noses

and ran, Jaap scrambling up the bank and Frans and Dirk running in the other direction.

"It's a skunk!" Dirk laughed. "And Snip took a direct hit!"

Frans laughed too. "Poor Snip. But it's better than being bitten. Skunks can be mean when they're cornered!"

Jaap didn't understand at all. He had some idea what a skunk was, but he'd never seen one—or smelled one. Frans patiently explained that every skunk had a gland which contained an extremely smelly fluid that it used to defend itself. Whenever it was cornered by a human being or by some animal it would squirt the offensive liquid at its enemy.

It was a perfectly good weapon as Snip found out. The poor dog tried to wash his nose in the snow, but that didn't get rid of the stench. The boys felt sorry for the dog, but time and again they burst out laughing at the dog's strange, frustrated antics. Dirk especially roared with laughter, but he hadn't forgotten their prey. After a while he asked, "So how are we going to get him?"

"Get who?" asked Frans puzzled.

"That skunk of course!"

"We're not going to get him. You want to crawl into that culvert and get a squirt of that stinking stuff? Besides, do you plan to drag that skunk out with your bare hands? We better get started for home right away. It's almost dark, and we have a long ways to go."

Dirk began to put up an argument. He didn't want the hunt to come to an end yet. But Frans turned and started walking toward home. He had been startled by the fact that it was already so dark. When he glanced up at the sky, he realized why. Earlier the sun had been shining, but now the sky was completely overcast. Frans knew that they were in for a snowstorm.

"Let's go, guys! We have to get home before it starts to snow," he warned.

"Oh, we'll make it," replied Dirk. "We can head straight for the mill. It won't take us nearly as long to get back."

"Straight for the mill? The mill won't help us if we can't see it!" snorted Frans. He was a little nervous and also ashamed that he hadn't shown more sense. They should have been home already.

Dirk fell silent; though bold and outspoken, he usually gave in to his older brother Frans, who, he realized very well, had a lot more sense than he did.

They cut straight across the white fields. Frans was pretty sure about the direction. They hurried as fast as they could. Jaap had trouble keeping up, but he wasn't about to admit it. Snip was no longer looking for tracks; the skunk had spoiled it for him.

CHAPTER VIII

Lost in a Blizzard

Suddenly a white snowflake floated down before Frans's eyes. Then there was a second and a third. And suddenly there were hundreds—thousands of them. The snowstorm had caught them before they were halfway home!

"Didn't I tell you?" growled Frans. He wanted to go even faster, but when he looked at Jaap, he realized he couldn't. Jaap was moving as fast as he could.

Within minutes they were in a blizzard, and visibility was almost zero. Soon Frans was no longer sure they were going the right way. Everything looked so different; all the familiar signs were blotted out by the snow.

Where were they? Frans had lost all sense of direction, but he didn't say anything to Dirk and Jaap because they trusted his judgment. He was the oldest and was expected to look after the others. But what if he got lost?

They struggled on through the blinding snow. Their high spirits of the afternoon soon gave way to anxiety. Dirk and Jaap sensed that things were going badly. For a long time nobody said a word.

Frans was growing frantic; he tried his best to figure out which way they were going. If he could only find signs of a farm or a familiar landmark by which to orient himself! But he saw nothing. Their world had suddenly become very small.

The wind had changed too. First it had been blowing right into his face, later it had veered to their backs, and now it was blowing from another direction. Or . . . Frans panicked. Maybe the wind had stayed the same and they had been going around in circles! His heart began to race, but he dared not voice his fear.

Then Dirk pointed to the ground in front of them. "Look," he said, obviously relieved, "there were people here. And not very long ago. Let's shout; maybe they'll hear us."

But the footprints only confirmed Frans's fear. "Those are our footprints," he said lamely. "We've walked in a big circle."

The others looked at him in amazement. "That's impossible; we were going in a straight line!" replied Dirk, stubbornly. He walked to the half-covered footsteps, inspected them and planted his foot in one of them. "You're right; they are ours," he admitted.

They were lost in a blizzard, tired and discouraged.

Jaap Roseboom remained calm. The Jewish boy had seen so much during the last few years and had faced so many dangers, that he didn't easily give way to despair. But he was so tired, that he sat down in the snow to take a breather.

Frans had to think; there had to be a way out. He noticed that Dirk, less of a hero than he pretended to be, was fighting back tears. He saw Jaap sitting on the ground, exhausted. He was reminded of a story he had once read about Napoleon's invasion of Russia. On their way back from Moscow, as they crossed the endless expanse of snow covered fields, exhausted soldiers would often sit down for a brief rest and before they knew it they were dead.

Ah, that was nonsense. The temperature was only just below zero. They weren't in any danger. If only there was a light around somewhere! But everything was dark by law. Frans had no idea at all which way was home.

Suddenly he thought about praying. Only God could help them now.

Then he heard that familiar, dull roar again in the distance, the same sound he had heard the other night. It was rapidly coming closer. Frans realized what it was: Allied bombers on their way to Germany on a bombing mission.

Shortly thereafter the German anti-aircraft batteries opened up. He could tell which direction the sound was coming from and he also knew where the installations were. He thought for a moment to decide which way to go.

Snip also began to act up. The snow had washed off most of the stench, and his nose was returning to normal. He was obviously becoming bored standing around in the middle of nowhere getting cold. He wanted to go home and couldn't understand Frans's dawdling. He barked loudly to get the boys' attention. Then he started off by himself, came back again, and trotted off again, seemingly trying to get the boys to follow him. He was going in the same direction, Frans noticed, that he had just decided on. They may have been lost, but apparently Snip was not.

"We'll follow Snip," Frans decided. "He'll lead us home."

"Right, Snip is the best tracking dog in the whole country!" Dirk boasted loudly. All at once he had forgotten his despair.

The terrier never hesitated. They followed him across fields and ditches, through barbed wire and underbrush. Frans was now sure they were going in the right direction. The wind had died but it was still snowing steadily, huge fluffy flakes. Before long, they were caked with snow. Snip, too, sometimes blended right into the snowy landscape, but every so often he would shake himself clean.

The dog was going too fast; Jaap just couldn't keep up. Fortunately Frans had a piece of rope in his pocket, so he fastened it to Snip's collar. Now he could control the dog's speed.

The going was pretty slow; they were tired, hungry and cold, but at least they had regained hope. The anti-aircraft guns had fallen silent because the airplanes had passed out of range. The boys were surrounded by a snowy darkness.

Suddenly they came to a wide ditch that cut through the middle of the field. Frans and Dirk recognized it instantly and shouted excitedly. That was the main water way draining into the canal. If they turned right and followed it, they would eventually end up at the Kanaaldijk. Then they would have to backtrack a ways to get home. That involved quite a detour. It would be much quicker if they could cross the ditch and follow Snip home.

But the ditch was very wide. They had crossed it earlier but that had been in broad daylight and without snow. They had been able to find a good place to jump, but it was much more complicated now. The water was covered by a thin sheet of ice with a layer of snow on top of it. They had to be very careful.

It was easy for Snip. Frans dropped the rope and the dog quickly bounded across the ditch.

Frans hesitated. He looked around for a better place. Then he descended the bank to the edge of the water. He launched himself and just managed to reach the other side, but he had to grab a handful of weeds not to slide back into the water. He scrambled onto the bank, feeling quite pleased with himself.

Dirk of course had his own ideas about how to jump the ditch. "You've got to take a run at it!" he shouted. "Look!" He walked back about ten meters, turned, took a run and jumped from the top of the bank. But just as he pushed off, his foot slid out from under him. He landed on his rump, slid unceremoniously down the bank and ended up in the ditch. Seconds later, he too, scrambled up the bank, assisted by Frans, but he was soaked to his waist.

"Well, you did it again!" said Frans angrily. "You little know-it-all. Now you smell worse than Snip!"

Dirk, always ready with a retort otherwise, kept quiet this time. He'd done it again; would he never learn?

Jaap hesitated. He had to get across somehow, but he was dead tired and didn't think he could make it.

Frans stood on the other side encouraging him. "Do it the way I did it, Jaap. You'll be all right! I'll catch you."

Jaap carefully slid down the bank, selected a good spot, and got ready to jump. Suddenly his courage returned. So what if he got wet. He was among friends; they wouldn't laugh at him or betray him. That was all that mattered!

Then he jumped, but his legs failed him. He just didn't have enough strength after what he'd been through. Frans grabbed his arms, but that didn't keep him from getting wet feet. Still, he had done much better than Dirk.

Dirk had recovered his bravado and huffed, "See, my way worked just as well."

Frans snorted coldly but didn't reply. He whistled for Snip who immediately came charging back. Frans grabbed the end of the rope and they set off again. "You guys better stay back a ways. Snip has to be able to pick up the scent. Your smell will overpower his nose, and we'll get lost for sure."

Frans was only kidding, but the boys automatically hung back. Dirk and Jaap's feet were sloshing in their shoes and their feet ached with cold. Though happy to get across the ditch, Frans wasn't pleased with himself. He was thinking about home. His parents would be very worried. And it was his fault because he was the oldest. He would probably be punished for staying out too late.

They were now on familiar ground. Despite the darkness and the thick blanket of snow, Frans and Dirk began to recognize familiar landmarks. Then at last they saw the dark silhouette of the windmill in the distance, standing like a lonely sentinel. Frans untied the rope from Snip's collar and the dog, anxious to get home, darted off toward the mill.

"At least they'll know we're coming," explained Frans. Despite his anxieties and the prospect of punishment, he was very relieved to be home again. They entered the yard and were just about to head for the house when Frans spotted a ray of light through a crack under the mill door. Apparently his father was still working.

He turned and walked toward the mill, followed by the others. Dirk wanted to go in right away, but Frans told him, "First clean yourself up a little; we're dirty enough as it is!" They shook and brushed the snow off before entering. Then they slipped inside and closed the door behind them to keep the snow out.

Mulders was just finishing his chores. When he saw the three boys an odd expression came to his face. He looked relieved and dismayed at the same time. Frans first thought it was because of Dirk's condition, but the next moment he saw the real reason why.

There were two other men in the mill—men with rifles. They were the same two National Guardsmen they had seen cycling through the fields a few days before. The two men looked surprised and also suspicious, especially when they saw Jaap.

Dirk was just about to say something but his father beat him to it. "I can't use you here! Get out!" he barked. Confused, they opened the door and stumbled back outside.

"Can you beat that? He threw us out of our own mill!" complained Dirk.

"Hush! They're Guardsmen."

Dirk still didn't catch on. "We didn't do anything," he whined.

Frans turned to him and hissed, "Don't be so dense. Have you forgotten about Jaap? Maybe that's why those two guys are here."

It finally sank in. Dirk blushed and quickly made his way to the house, as far from those dangerous Guardsmen as possible.

Jaap didn't need an explanation. He had been hounded and persecuted so much that he had seen the danger immediately. A frightened, almost animal look had come into his eyes. He wanted to flee, back into the blizzard, but then he would have to leave his friends behind, and they were the only people who cared about him.

Frans sensed something of the boy's struggle. "You better come with us; we'll take care of you," he said gently, and he put his arm around the boy's shoulder.

Mother and Nel were in the living room, obviously worried, but when the three boys came into the room, they immediately relaxed. "Am I happy to see you! You really gave us a fright. What happened to you, Dirk?"

"Fell in the water," Dirk replied sheepishly.

"That's dreadful! You look a fright," grumbled Mother. But she seemed preoccupied with something else.

"What are those Guardsmen doing in the mill?" Frans asked.

His mother started. "Did they see you?"

"Yes, Mother. We went in because we saw a light burning, but Dad kicked us out."

"And rightly so! You can't trust that rabble. Too bad they spotted Jaap! They've been here for over two hours already. They said they had to inspect the supplies in the mill, and they asked your father some questions about the black market. Of course, he didn't know anything about that. He explained that he was here to help people, but not for black market prices. But they just hang around and keep asking questions and poking around in the supplies. I went over there a couple of times to see what was going on, so I know what they're up to. When the blizzard came, they said they wanted to stay until it had passed. They pretend they're not looking for anything special, but I don't trust them for a moment. They're up to something, I just know."

Mother told Dirk to get cleaned up and then went to fetch him some clean clothes. Jaap followed Dirk to the pantry because he had to wash his feet too.

They had leftovers for supper. Frans and Dirk had enormous appetites, but Jaap hardly touched his food. He was just too tired and he was very nervous about the two Guardsmen in the mill.

Just as they were finishing, there was a rap on the window pane. They sat bolt upright, but then they heard Father's reassuring voice. "Open up, they're gone!"

Mother smiled. "I locked the door—just to be on the safe side," she explained. She quickly crossed the floor to open the door.

Mulders looked very relieved. "Well, those thugs are gone. I finally told them to leave. It's still snowing but that won't kill them. Mother, why don't you pour me a cup of your phony coffee." He sank back in his chair and told them what had happened. The boys already knew the main details, but they listened closely anyway.

Mulders noticed the hunted look in Jaap's eyes, and he tried to calm him down. He explained that the two policemen were just a couple of bunglers. All their ravings and rantings didn't mean a thing and they had found nothing.

"Were you boys startled when I barked at you like that?" he asked, laughing. "But it was the only way. I had heard Snip barking just a few seconds before, and I guessed you would probably come toward the mill, so I had to do something. I didn't want to give them a chance to have a good look at Jaap. At any rate, all's well that ends well. But now you boys better hit the hay."

That night Jaap slept on a cot in Frans and Dirk's room. He was obviously pleased; it gave him a feeling of security he hadn't had in a long time.

When the three boys had gone to bed, Mulders talked things over with his wife, Nel and Dries, who had just come home. He wasn't as self-assured as he had pretended. He was convinced that the Guardsmen had been sent to spy on him. They had also asked him who Jaap was. Mulders had merely shrugged his shoulders and told them that he was probably one of their school friends, but he wasn't sure whether they believed him. In any event, the family would have to be very careful, because the enemy could and would strike a blow at any time. They decided it would be best that Jaap move on as quickly as possible.

CHAPTER IX

The Search

The next day Mulders took immediate action. He sent Dries to Uncle Janus, who promised that Jaap would be moved within three days. He couldn't go any sooner, so they would have to make do until then.

Mulders wasn't one to get scared easily, but a sixth sense alerted him to danger. So he fixed a hiding place for Jaap in case of a search.

They decided on the lumber shed. A large supply of beams was neatly stacked against the wall. Mr. Mulders and Dries worked all afternoon, restacking the beams so that there was a space inside just large enough for one person. Jaap could crawl in through one end of the stack and the entrance could then be plugged by inserting a short, heavy beam in the opening. With the beam in place, the secret hiding place was completely invisible.

When they were finished, Mulders called Dirk, Frans and Jaap. He showed them the hiding place, and Jaap tried it out. He told Jaap to head for the lumbershed at the first sign of trouble.

Dirk and Frans were very impressed, but Jaap took it all in stride without showing any emotion. He was used to this.

Dirk assured him that he would tackle anyone who got near his friend, but his father snapped that he should do nothing but keep his big mouth shut.

Nothing happened the next day. Then came New Year's Eve. Everyone was in a holiday mood, especially Frans, Dirk and Jaap. Mother was planning to make *oliebollen* that afternoon, and that evening they would be allowed to stay up until midnight. There was still snow on the ground, so the three friends decided to make a snowman next to the lumbershed.

They had just finished their creation when they were called for lunch. They were all rosy cheeked with exertion and excitement, and they had tremendous appetites.

After lunch Mother started to deep-fry her *oliebollen*. The boys hung around the kitchen in the hope of getting one or two, but Mother finally chased them out. The three boys were getting in the way.

So they went outside again. At first they didn't know what to do, but then Frans had an idea. He was pretty good at clay modelling. So he took some snow and began to change the snowman's features. Before long, the snowman had been reshaped in the image of their archenemy, Dreumel. Dirk recognized it immediately and burst out laughing.

Jaap looked puzzled; he didn't know who Dreumel was, so the two boys explained. One thing led to another. Frans stepped off twenty paces from the snowman and started making a supply of snowballs. Dirk caught on right away. "Ah, target practice!" he shouted excitedly, as he quickly started producing his own arsenal.

Soon a barrage of snowballs hailed down on the make-believe Dreumel. Not every snowball was on target, but at last the head toppled from the body.

"Yippee! He's dead!" shouted Dirk.

Frans, however, was overcome by a strange feeling. It was only a game, of course; yet every time he threw a snowball he had the nagging feeling that this was what he wanted to do to the real Dreumel. And, judging from Dirk's reaction, he probably felt the same way.

"Come on, let's put the head back on," said Dirk. "You fix up his face again, Frans."

Frans repressed the strange feeling and began to sculpture a new head, one that looked even more like the real Dreumel.

They were right next to the lumbershed and the wall of the shed was splattered with snow. Dad and Dries were working inside; the constant whine of the circular saw drowned out every other noise.

Just then Nel burst around the corner of the shed; she looked like she'd seen a ghost. "Quick," she shouted. "Jaap has to hide! There's a police van coming down the Kanaaldijk!"

The boys froze. They had become so caught up in their game that they had forgotten everything else. Jaap was the first to react. He dashed for the shed. Fortunately the door faced away from the dike, so he couldn't be spotted from there.

Seconds later the circular saw stopped, and Frans and Dirk could hear the van approaching the house. Nel walked back to the house as calmly as possible. Under no circumstances should she look suspicious.

Intuitively Frans reacted the same way; he said to Dirk, "Come on, let's build an igloo. We have to act as if there's nothing unusual going on."

He walked toward a snowdrift at the corner of the shed. Dirk didn't fully understand what was going on, but he obediently followed Frans to the corner.

The police van had pulled up in front of the mill and three uniformed men jumped out. Their leader had the rank of brigadier, a rank he had earned for being a member of the N.S.B. The other two were ordinary officers. These two men genuinely resented being used by the Germans to do their dirty work for them, but they lacked the courage to refuse and resign from the force or to go into hiding. The brigadier swaggered across the yard with an arrogant strut; he evidently enjoyed what he was doing. He marched to the front door of the house, opened it without knocking, and walked inside.

Mrs. Mulders had seen him coming and had time to compose herself. "What do you think you're doing?" she demanded calmly.

"I've got a warrant to search the premises," replied the brigadier weightily, waving a document in her face.

"Go ahead. There isn't much to search and nothing to find, but suit yourself." She was amazed at how calm she sounded.

"We know otherwise! There are refugees here!" snapped the Nazi sympathizer.

Mrs. Mulders merely shrugged her shoulders and went back to the kitchen to knead some more dough. But her hands were shaking, and Nel, who was helping her, was pale as a ghost.

"Officer Bakker, you go outside and keep an eye on the mill. Timmer, you take the upstairs and I'll take the downstairs." The two officers obeyed silently, and the brigadier proceeded directly to the kitchen.

"Well, well, making *oliebollen* no less! No shortage here, is there?" he said with mock cheerfulness, but he got no reply from either Mrs. Mulders or Nel. Mrs. Mulders wanted to say something but decided it was better not to antagonize him.

There was nothing in the kitchen, so the brigadier turned his attention to the other rooms. Meanwhile, Mrs. Mulders racked her brain whether there was anything in the house or the mill that might betray Jaap's presence. No, she decided, there was nothing. She had cleaned up the room in the top of the mill herself the day before and there was nothing in the house either.

Then she looked at Nel; she was shaking like a leaf and was on the verge of tears.

"Hush, child, everything will be all right," she soothed.

But Nel shook her head vehemently. "No, and it's my fault!" she whispered, as the tears sprang from her eyes. "This morning I cleaned up in the boys' room but instead of putting away Jaap's bed, I simply remade it. The officer upstairs will notice right away that there's a stranger in the house."

Mrs. Mulders almost broke down on the spot. How could Nel have been so negligent! She knew the bed had to be put away during the daytime. But when she saw how close Nel was to total collapse she decided against the reprimand.

"Maybe it'll turn out all right," she sighed. "The Lord will show the way." Her hands went back to the dough but her thoughts rose to Almighty God in heaven.

Her mother's apparent confidence strengthened Nel. She wiped her eyes and went back to work. The brigadier came back into the kitchen, looking sorely disappointed because he hadn't found anything. Shortly thereafter Officer Timmer also came into the kitchen. There was no way to describe how Mrs. Mulders and Nel felt at that moment. This was it.

"Anything to report, Timmer?"

"There's nobody upstairs, Brigadier. I went through everything with a fine tooth comb."

"Hmm, I see. You saw nothing suspicious, no indication there might be somebody up there?"

"Nothing suspicious to report, Brigadier," came his steady reply, but, very briefly, something glinted in his eyes. Mrs. Mulders, who was standing right across from him, just caught the fleeting gleam.

But the brigadier noticed nothing. He relapsed into thought, debating whether to investigate the upstairs himself. He knew that these two officers could not be completely trusted. They were indecisive men, who just didn't seem to understand the new age and the deliverance brought by their brothers from across the border.

No, he concluded, he'd better not. Timmer wouldn't dare withhold information from him. And if he went upstairs and found nothing, the man would just laugh behind his back. Anyway, it was much more likely that any fugitives would be hidden either in the mill or in the lumbershed. He had been tipped off about refugees here, and he'd been in this kind of a situation before; nobody was going to pull the wool over his eyes!

He turned abruptly and left the house, followed by Officer Timmer. They had only just closed the door behind them and Mrs. Mulders ran up the stairs, to Frans and Dirk's bedroom. Nel followed right on her heels.

When they entered the room, they got the surprise of their lives. The cot had disappeared! The two extra blankets had been placed on Frans and Dirk's beds, the pillow was on top of Frans's and the mattress had been placed at the back of the clothes closet.

"So you put it away after all!" exclaimed Mrs. Mulders.

"No, I didn't," Nel reassured her. "He . . . Timmer must have done that."

Mrs. Mulders was suddenly reminded of Timmer's words: "Nothing suspicious to report." She recalled the glint in his eyes. Suddenly she felt infinitely grateful, not only toward the police officer, but especially toward God who had made everything right.

In the meantime, Officer Bakker had been pacing up and down. He was just going through the motions, and his heart wasn't really in it. A nasty business, he reflected, all this persecution. He was slowly beginning to hate himself. If it weren't for his wife and children, he would have quit long ago. But then he would have ended up in Germany himself. And he wasn't very keen on that. Ah well, he hoped they would draw a blank this time. He knew that Timmer was of the same mind; this persecution and murder of human beings revolted him too.

He decided to take a walk around the mill and the lumber-shed, not to search, mind, but just to kill some time.

The circular saw was whining away again. Mulders knew exactly what was going on but pretended he didn't know anything about the police visit. Jaap was hidden inside the beams. Safely? Well, only time would tell. Dries had shifted a couple of bags full of sawdust and put them right next to the short beam that plugged the access to the hiding place. They hoped everything would be all right, but they were worried.

Outside, Frans and Dirk seemed to be engrossed in the task of building an igloo, but their thoughts, too, were elsewhere.

Officer Bakker came around the corner of the lumbershed. He thought about going inside and chatting with the miller for a while but decided against it. He would do what he was told, but that was all.

He stared down at the two boys for a while. He knew them pretty well, he had often seen them in town. Just innocent kids, who were so caught up in their games that they had no time for world drama.

Then he saw the snowman. At first it looked just like any other snowman, but then he looked again. The snowman was almost lifesize and its right arm was raised in a Nazi salute. Suddenly Bakker recognized who it was, that wide mouth, those jowls, those eyes . . .

Then he burst out laughing. Of course, it was Dreumel, the guy who always came to the police station for secret chats with Brigadier Nelissen. It was his spitting image. But it was better if the brigadier didn't see it! There was no telling what he might do to the boys.

He gave the snowman a shove and that was the end of that. But the expression on his face had changed. While only a moment ago he had looked depressed now he was grinning. He walked back to the house and was met by Brigadier Nelissen and Officer Timmer.

"Did you find anything?" demanded Brigadier Nelissen.

"Nothing at all, Brigadier!" reported Officer Bakker.

"All right then, let's go to the mill. You stay outside again, Bakker, and we'll go through the mill. Keep your eyes open."

The mill was given a thorough going over, but without results. Nelissen was becoming surly. He had been promised success, but it didn't look like it now. His face drawn and angry, he came down the stairs to the main floor.

The only place left was the lumbershed. Beyond that there was no place to hide out. Two boys were playing in the snow, seemingly oblivious to what was going on. They never even gave the business a second thought.

It looked a little too contrived, too artificial, decided the suspicious policeman. Something was wrong; it was just too peaceful. He decided to do a thorough job on the lumbershed, even if he had to turn the building upside down.

"Let's go," he snapped. "We're all going inside and we're not leaving a stone unturned."

Mulders and Dries were still busy working. They looked up in surprise, but they didn't seem at all worried when the policemen came in. They just went back to their work.

Nelissen walked up to the miller and demanded, "Are you hiding fugitives?"

He couldn't compete with the noise of the circular saw, so Mulders pretended he hadn't understood. He only shook his head and said, "Sorry, we can't stop now, we're much too busy. Go talk to my wife!"

Nelissen tried again. "We're here to search the premises!" he shouted at the top of his voice. Mulders decided he'd better cooperate. Feigning surprise, he looked wide-eyed at the brigadier, then simply shrugged his shoulders and said, "Go ahead."

The brigadier was getting nastier by the minute. He expected people to show him respect and even fear, but this man refused to pay any attention to him at all. And that son of his with those defiant eyes—he'd like to pin his ears back.

"Shut down that saw; it's driving me crazy!" he roared. When Mulders made no move to shut it down he threw the switch himself.

Gradually the saw came to a stop. The irritated brigadier told his officers to get busy. There were boards, logs, beams and mounds of sawdust everywhere—all obstacles that slowed down the search.

Mulders quickly saw that Officers Bakker and Timmer only made a show of looking, but Nelissen was a real fanatic, who made up for his subordinates' lack of zeal. Nevertheless, he discovered nothing unusual, and that made him madder still.

Finally, everything had been thoroughly checked except the large pile of beams against the wall. The brigadier didn't really believe that someone was hidden under it but there might have been a secret trapdoor or something. In any event, his frustration had made him unreasonable.

"Clear away that pile of beams!" he yelled.

Mulders started, but quickly regained his composure. "They're much too heavy to move, and I've got work to do," he said. "If you want to move them, fine, go ahead, but I'm not going to help you in your folly."

Nelissen turned beet red but knew that he had pushed Mulders as far as he could. So he ordered Bakker and Timmer to move the beams. Mulders and Dries could hardly hide their anxiety. Jaap, who could hear everything of course, was trembling from fear as he saw his doom approaching.

Outside, Frans and Dirk didn't know what the score was but they were becoming restless. It was taking so long. The longer the searchers stayed inside, the greater the chance that Jaap would be discovered.

Finally Dirk couldn't stand it anymore. He started shaking with fear, impatience, and fury. He had to do something not to explode. He wanted to run into the shed, grab the officers by the throat and drag them outside.

In a fit of uncontrollable fury he picked up a snowball and heaved it at the side of the lumbershed. It thudded against the wooden wall and right away Dirk reached for a second. He hurled it with everything he had, then reached for a third, and a fourth and a fifth . . . He wasn't even aiming any more. The shed was so big he couldn't miss. He had to vent his fear and frustration.

Nelissen turned at the quick succession of thuds. His anger made way for suspicion. What was going on out there? He walked to the side window, opened it and looked out. A split second later a snowball exploded in his face.

CHAPTER X

The Brigadier in Pursuit

The explosion was followed by hundreds of stars dancing and whirling before his eyes. Emitting a beastly shout, he pulled back his head, slammed the window and rushed for the door.

Dirk had thrown the snowball without any particular target in mind. Not until he heard the brigadier's bloodcurdling shriek did he realize what he had done. For a few seconds he just stood there, paralyzed. Then he saw the enraged brigadier come hurtling around the corner of the shed straight toward him.

"Get out of here, Dirk!" yelled Frans. That did it. Dirk bolted around the other corner of the building. But the brigadier was no slouch. Every stride narrowed the gap between him and his prey.

Dirk had no time to think; he just took off, not really knowing where to go. He just wanted to stay out of the brigadier's clutches as long as possible. But then he realized that he was heading straight for the wood pond filled with logs. The pond was covered by a thin layer of ice, but he knew the ice wouldn't bear his weight.

Poor Dirk was driven by panic, and the panic grew as the

shouts and snarls behind him drew closer. Soon he felt the brigadier steaming down his neck, and the only way out was the pond.

He made up his mind: across the pond. In all likelihood the heavyset policeman wouldn't try to follow him there. Frans and Dirk had played this game before, but that was in the summertime. They would leap from one log to the next until they reached firm ground on the other side of the pond.

Their father frowned on it, and their mother always scolded them when she saw them at it. They had both had the misfortune of ending up in the water—Dirk twice, Frans once. And they had both been punished for it. But on a warm summer day the temptation was sometimes just too much.

There was no such temptation now. The water was icy cold, and the floating logs were covered with ice and snow. Normally, Dirk wouldn't think of trying to do what he was about to do. But what choice did he have? It was the only way.

So he leaped and landed on the first log. Okay so far. He just managed to retain his balance. Then he ran the length of the log to a point where he could simply step onto the next one.

Again, so far so good. He had reached the second log without mishap. The third was butted right up to it; so he gradually made his way to the center of the pond. He just had to be very careful not to slip, for then he'd go down under.

The logs were beginning to heave up and down a bit as the ice between them broke. Occasionally the water would lap over the top of the logs.

The brigadier had halted at the edge of the pond. He was beside himself because it looked like the little devil would make good his escape. But he wasn't about to go after Dirk, not this way.

Suddenly Snip came charging around the corner of the building. Nobody knew where he came from, but he clearly sensed that the policeman had something evil in store for his little master. He jumped up against the brigadier's legs, yelping and snapping fiercely.

The mad dog's unjustified attack made something snap inside the brigadier's head. He aimed several kicks at the dog, but Snip was too quick for him, and each time he resumed his attacks.

Mulders and Dries emerged from the lumbershed with the two officers. Mulders slowly walked toward the pond, wondering how to rescue Dirk from this predicament. Timmer and Bakker were almost choking with glee. To see the Brigadier bombarded by a snowball had been the highlight of their careers. Secretly they hoped that Dirk would escape.

The brigadier suddenly realized how preposterous he looked. Naturally his subordinates were laughing behind his back, and that miserable cur had no respect at all for his Germanic dignity!

Just then, before zeroing in on the next log, Dirk glanced back. Nelissen thought he detected a self-satisfied, smug look on the boy's face. That did it; that was the last straw. Without thinking, he committed himself to pursuit across the pond. He came down hard on the first log, and for a second it looked like he would go under, but he managed to regain his balance and immediately jumped onto the second log.

The brigadier was strong and agile. He didn't bother walking the length of the log so that he could step onto the next one. He went straight on and jumped from the first log right onto the second and the third. That way, he rapidly closed the gap between himself and Dirk.

"Dirk, get out of there; you'll drown!" shouted his father.

Probably the boy never heard it. He was propelled by fear, fear of that dreadful monster behind him, that Nazi sympathizer, who, when he got hold of him, would probably flog him and beat him black and blue.

"Stay where you are," roared Nelissen. His words, of

course, had the opposite effect and made the boy even more reckless. But still the brigadier came on, and still he was gaining ground, or at least logs.

Snip ran around to the far side of the pond. Frans looked like he had apoplexy. Dries was clenching his fists and his knuckles were turning white. If that traitor touched one hair on his little brother's head, he'd . . .

Mulders quickly followed Snip to the other side of the pond. For their part, Bakker and Timmer didn't seem in a hurry to help their superior. Their faces were expressionless masks.

Dirk was just past the middle of the pond and had about a three meter jump on the brigadier. The brigadier suddenly saw his chance; with one long leap he could get to within a meter of the fleeing Dirk and that would be the end of the chase. Still spurred by blind wrath, he didn't calculate the risks. He pushed off, sailed gracefully through the air and came down on target, but . . . scratch one brigadier. He disappeared completely under the surface of the water.

He didn't stay down long. The forward momentum of the jump had carried him right under the ice, but the brigadier was a very determined person, and he butted his head against the ice until he broke it.

It scared Dirk half out of his wits. He looked back to see what was going on, forgetting to watch where he was going. This was his downfall. He slipped, tried to right himself . . . too late. Down he sank into the water, but he managed to keep his upper body out of the water by hanging onto the log. Shaking with cold and fright he struggled back onto the log. Seconds later he reached the other shore, where his father met him to take care of him.

For Nelissen it wasn't over yet. He grabbed hold of the thin end of the log so that his clothes wouldn't drag him down, but he'd never be able to clamber onto the log. His uniform was an obstacle even under the best circumstances. But he had enough presence of mind and dignity to straighten his cap. After all, it was the uniform that gave him stature. He didn't realize how preposterous he looked; his cap was covered with ice and snow.

"Get the ladder from the shed!" yelled Mulders, who still had his hands full with his son Dirk.

Dries ran to the shed, followed by the two officers. Dries lifted the ladder down from the wall and started back to the pond. Bakker and Timmer had joined him in the shed, but, had it been up to them, they would have gone off and left the brigadier to fend for himself. Dries noticed the officers' lack of enthusiasm and he himself had enjoyed the dunking the brigadier got, but he couldn't very well let him drown. And, anyway, what would happen to Dirk if he did?

The minute the two officers were safely in the shed, their behavior changed completely. Until now they had looked on with stoney faces, but suddenly they burst out in uncontrollable laughter.

"I knew that would happen the minute he went up to the

pond; I saw it coming!" roared Bakker, wiping away his tears.

Timmer grinned broadly. "Maybe now some of that pro-German zeal will cool off," he chuckled.

When they had had their fun, they realized they had to do something, even if just for appearance's sake. So they each grabbed a board and ran outside.

Meanwhile Dries had returned to the pond with the ladder, and his father joined him. Nelissen was still clutching the end of the log but he was so cold and stiff by now that he was incapable of helping himself.

Dries was just about to shove the ladder out over the logs, but his father intervened. "You take Dirk inside. Tell Mother to put some dry clothes on him and to make sure he's out of sight when I bring in victim number two."

Dries and Dirk left immediately. Mulders slid the ladder out over the logs to a point where it was directly in front of the unfortunate brigadier. Gingerly, the miller edged out onto the rungs toward the victim.

Frans was unable to keep up his act of building the igloo. He was on the other side of the lumbershed and couldn't see a thing. So he ran to his father to see if he could use any help. He was joined by the two officers, who had composed themselves in the meantime.

But Mulders could manage all by himself. He had reached the end of the ladder and grabbed the brigadier's collar. There was little the brigadier could do to help in the rescue operation, but at last Mulders succeeded in hauling the man out onto the end of the ladder.

As rescue operations go, it was pretty shaky. Nelissen was heavy, his clothes probably even heavier, and his high boots filled to the brim with water. Besides, the ladder wasn't very sturdy and the supporting logs shaky at best. At one point Mulders almost joined the brigadier in the water, quite unintentionally of course, but he just managed to regain his balance. At the other end, the two officers held the ladder down to prevent it from turning over or tipping up.

In the end it worked. Mulders slowly made his way backward across the ladder, dragging the semi-conscious, not very official looking brigadier along with him. Bakker and Timmer looked on with feigned concern.

At last the shipwrecked brigadier and his rescuer made it back to solid ground. The miller showered the poor brigadier with genuine concern and compassion. He quickly ushered Nelissen back to the house.

Meanwhile, a great deal had been going on inside. Mother and Nel had been shocked out of their wits upon seeing Dirk, dripping and pale, escorted in by his older brother. Dries told them what had happened. Mother and daughter had been completely unaware of what was happening because the mill and the shed were between the house and the pond. They had been very concerned for Jaap but had deliberately refrained from going to the shed. That might have looked suspicious.

And now suddenly this! But Mother quickly recovered her wits. There wasn't a moment to lose. She quickly rubbed Dirk dry, gave him some dry clothes and packed him off to bed with a hot water bottle. Just to be sure, she locked the bedroom door and put the key in her apron pocket. Nelissen was not going to carry off her son.

She had only just finished with all this, when her husband came in escorting the brigadier. The reception he got this time was entirely different than other times. Whereas previously Mrs. Mulders had been cold and disapproving, she now radiated concern for this unfortunate creature. The kitchen stove was fired up and the victim placed right in front of it to help him overcome his shock.

Mulders and the brigadier were about the same size, so Nelissen could borrow some of her husband's underwear and clothing. He was left alone in the kitchen to dry himself and get dressed.

When he had finished, he resumed his position in front of the stove and gradually regained his senses. Nel prepared a warm drink for him and even gave him the first *oliebol*. All the while, Dirk's name never cropped up.

At first Nelissen was withdrawn and suspicious. He was sure that everybody was quietly laughing at him, and so he stewed about what he should do. With his uniform gone he had lost most of his spunk. Gradually it began to dawn on him how preposterous he had acted.

All right, so those kids had been throwing snowballs at the shed. That wasn't against the law. If he hadn't put his head through the window nothing would have happened. That rascal hadn't aimed at him directly. In fact, he had already released the snowball when the window opened. Still, he wouldn't mind giving that kid a good thrashing or even lock him up in a cell for the night. But he shouldn't have been so asinine as to follow the kid across the pond; he should have just waited for him to come ashore.

He looked about angrily. What should he do now? Could he arrest the boy after his father had rescued him from the water, the mother had given him dry clothes, and the sister food and drink?

If only they had showed the slightest sign of disrespect, just a hint of a sneer, then he . . . But there was none of that. Mulders and Dries had left the house. Mrs. Mulders was busy feeding the fire. The daughter offered him a few more *oliebollen*. Officers Bakker and Timmer were sitting at the table also eating *oliebollen,* and seemed to have forgotten completely about the incident. It might be better, he reflected, to try to forget the whole thing, however humiliating it was. If he took any action now, he'd probably become the laughingstock of the whole town. And as far as the tips about refugees were concerned, he had discovered for himself that there was no truth to it.

Gradually, he worked himself into a better frame of mind.

He had good reason: it was pleasantly warm, he had had good care, his subordinates showed no sign of disrespect, there was no sign that the incident would work to his disadvantage.

Mrs. Mulders offered to wash and dry his uniform for him, but that was just too much. He decided to take it along as is. He promised that someone would deliver the borrowed clothes in a couple of days. He even thanked them for their assistance.

Half an hour later the police van left, much to the relief of the Mulders family, who fervently hoped they would never experience another New Year's Eve like this.

CHAPTER XI

New Year's Eve

Mr. Mulders and Dries had gone back to the workshop. The circular saw whined and chewed its way through the logs. Mulders had decided it was better to leave Nelissen in his wife's care; he was confident she could handle him.

Frans hung around the outside of the lumbershed and the mill, ready to alert his father to any new problems.

They hadn't touched the stack of beams lined up against the wall yet. Jaap must have been feeling anxious and confused. He had, of course, overheard the brigadier saying he wanted the whole pile cleared away.

Before they turned on the saw Dries had walked up to the beams. In an undertone he had said, "Hang in there, Jaap! Everything will be all right." There had been no reply. The boy must have been numb with fright.

The two men had gone back to work, but their thoughts were elsewhere. Mulders wondered what Nelissen would do next. He had made a fool of himself, and he was probably contemplating revenge even now. True, they had taken care of him to the best of their abilities, but you could never predict what a Nazi sympathizer would do . . .

Frans burst into the shed. "Dad, they're gone!" he shouted.

Mulders shut down the saw. "What about Dirk?" he asked.

"He wasn't with them!" Frans laughed. "There was just the three of them."

Mulders and Dries ran outside. It was already growing dark, but they could see the police van racing off in the distance.

"Thank God!" was the miller's genuine comment.

Mrs. Mulders and Nel joined them in the lumbershed. Mother was laughing, somewhat hysterically, and tears were running down her cheeks. She had held up pretty well under the ordeal, but now that the danger was past she suddenly realized how tense she had been. She went up to her husband and hung on his arm.

"Is Dirk okay?" Mulders asked. He knew the answer to that, but he couldn't resist asking anyway.

"Everything's okay," sighed his wife, much relieved. "I've locked him up in his room. I would never have turned over the key to the brigadier!"

"You've been a pure marvel," said Mulders in amazement. "You defused that crisis beautifully. I think you made a big impression on Nelissen. But I still don't trust that Nazi. Jaap Roseboom has to leave here as quickly as possible; it's just not safe anymore. But first we'll have to dig him out of his hiding place. I almost passed out when that brigadier said he wanted those beams cleared away!"

Walking back to the beams, Mulders removed the bags of sawdust Dries had placed against one end of the stack, removed the "key" from the hole and called, "Come on out, Jaap; the coast is clear!"

There was no reply and also no movement. Mulders became worried. Had the boy suffocated? Impossible; there were enough holes and cracks between the wood beams to let in fresh air. And yet . . .

Frans slipped into the hole and crawled through the narrow

corridor to where Jaap was supposed to be. He couldn't see anything so he groped about with his hands. Presently he reemerged. "He's not there, Dad!" They all looked at each other. How could that be?

"Jaap, where are you?" Mulders shouted.

"I'm coming!" came the reply from somewhere above them. Somehow he had made his way into the attic. He looked very pale, but he was relieved and happy.

"How did you get up there?" asked Mulders, flabbergasted.

So Jaap explained. While in hiding under the beams, he had overheard everything. He had almost fainted with fear when he heard the brigadier give orders to move the beams. Then something had happened that he hadn't understood, but he had heard the brigadier charge outside, shouting and cursing, and everybody else run after him. When they didn't come back right away, he had removed the "key" and crawled out. Then he had replaced the "key" and the sacks of sawdust and had darted up the ladder to the attic, which had already been checked by Nelissen. He had hidden under some tarps. He had just settled down when Dries and the two policemen had come back inside to fetch a ladder.

"Well done, Jaap!" said Mr. Mulders. "If they had come back inside, they wouldn't have looked for you on the attic floor. Well, it's time to lock up; I'm not going to do anymore work this year. Let's all go back inside and have a nice evening together."

It was completely dark outside; snow was falling again and the wind blew briskly. After they had secured the lumbershed and the mill, they went back to their warm, cozy living room.

It was the most unusual New Year's Eve they had ever celebrated. Any other time they would have gone to church, but not this time. Although Mulders had a hard time deciding, finally he advised against it. Jaap wouldn't be able to go along, so it was better that none of them went. Mr.

Mulders felt very sorry for the young boy who no longer had anybody to look after him. He was destined to be shipped from one place to the next, always only one step ahead of the Nazi bloodhounds. Tomorrow or the next day he would vanish from their lives, maybe permanently. So Mr. Mulders thought it better to spend at least one evening together and give him something to remember them by.

Gradually the wind picked up force and the gentle snowfall turned into a blizzard. That was all right with them, because now the likelihood that they would get visitors was very small. Just to be sure, however, Mr. Mulders securely locked all outside doors.

Dirk had come downstairs too. At first he pussyfooted around a bit, because he expected to be punished. But that didn't happen. Mr. Mulders told the others what had happened in the lumbershed when the police were searching the place, and Mrs. Mulders and Nel told about the cot that had somehow mysteriously vanished. For his part, Dirk confessed why he had started throwing snowballs in the first place. "It was an accident, you know. It really was!" he said heatedly.

His father began to laugh. "Well, it may have been an accident, but it was a fortunate one. Just then it looked like everything was going wrong in the lumbershed, but the snowball distracted the brigadier's attention from the beams. He was so beside himself he charged outside and practically jumped right into the pond!"

Everyone had a good laugh about that, including Dirk. Suddenly, instead of feeling like a culprit, he felt like a hero. But when the laughter died down, Mr. Mulders said, "The Lord was protecting us. We may say it was all accidental, but in reality He shaped the course of events. We've got good reason to thank Him for His faithfulness."

It turned out to be a cozy, relaxed evening together. Mother had spent quite a bit of time on supper: everyone got a cooked egg and, of course, several delicious *oliebollen*. She surprised them all with a jug of hot chocolate—real chocolate, not the imitation stuff you bought nowadays; she had been saving it for three years. It was a special treat for the kids but especially for Jaap, that poor, hounded orphan whom she had grown so attached to.

Jaap was quiet at first; he was still shaky. He knew that his days here were numbered and that he would soon be moved to a new location. But the good food, the warmth, and the company and cheerfulness of his friends made him forget his troubles. Before long he was laughing and joking with the rest of them.

Just this once the boys were allowed to stay up until midnight. Dirk was overjoyed. This was the first time ever for him. After what he had done that afternoon, he had expected to be punished, not spoiled and coddled. "You never know," he thought to himself. "But who's complaining?"

Later in the evening, Mr. Mulders began to tell stories and jokes about his earlier days with Janus Van Beveren. While his accounts were probably laced with a good deal of imagination, the kids found his stories very amusing and kept asking for more.

Later the discussion turned to the war, with Father and Dries doing most of the talking, while the others listened attentively. The German armies in Russia were taking a severe beating, even though they continued to resist stubbornly. Southern Italy had been taken by the Americans and the English. For all practical purposes, the Italians had already bowed out of the conflict, but their German "allies" now occupied most of the northern half of the peninsula and continued to fight almost to the last man.

At eleven o'clock Mrs. Mulders began to play the organ. Together they sang psalms and hymns and some patriotic songs. The latter Jaap knew very well, so he sang along, but he wasn't familiar with the psalms and hymns.

Toward midnight Mr. Mulders took the Bible down from

the shelf. Everyone gathered around and listened reverently as he read Psalm 90: "Lord, thou hast been our dwelling place in all generations." Then he led in prayer, thanking God for His protection and providence in the troubled year that lay behind them. He also prayed for the queen and asked the Lord to deliver the Dutch and other oppressed peoples from Hitler's yoke.

At twelve o'clock sharp they wished each other a happy new year and went to bed. All the others quickly dropped off to sleep, but Jaap stayed awake for a long, long time, reflecting on what had happened in the past, but especially on what he had experienced this New Year's Eve.

CHAPTER XII

A Message from Uncle Janus

Christmas vacation was over, and Frans and Dirk were back in school. Jaap had left; he had vanished from their lives just as suddenly as he had appeared. On the second of January Uncle Janus had picked him up and sent him to a new address.

Where? None of the Mulders knew. It was better that way, they realized. The only one who knew was Van Beveren. He had personally taken the boy to a distant farm. There were more fugitives there, and it was relatively safe. The farmer and his wife were excellent people, and so Van Beveren could safely assure the Mulders that Jaap would be all right, considering the circumstances.

Frans and Dirk regretted losing their friend, but they realized there was no other way. One of the Guardsmen had returned one day shortly after Jaap had been moved, ostensibly to find out the price of lumber, but really to have a quick look around. Mulders had quickly gotten rid of him, and the man hadn't seen anything suspicious, but it was clear that the Germans and their henchmen were keeping an eye on the place.

Officer Timmer had returned the clothes the brigadier had

borrowed. He had stayed for a cup of imitation coffee and had talked guardedly about this and that. Upon leaving, he had shaken Mrs. Mulders' hand and said, "Thanks for everything."

"It's you who should be thanked!" Mrs. Mulders had replied. She recalled the incident of the cot and the fact that Timmer hadn't betrayed them, but instead put the bed away.

The officer had smiled but said nothing. It hadn't been necessary; they had understood each other without further communication.

Life was back to normal; in reality, of course, it wasn't normal at all. Every night squadrons of English bombers crossed the Netherlands to carry out their raids in Germany. Every day, too, there were reports of terrible fighting in Russia, Italy and on nearly all other fronts. In addition, Dutch people were being arrested every day and herded together into concentration camps or executed on the spot. The rest, those who were relatively free, knew that there was no true liberty. In fact, the whole country was one giant concentration camp. And as the German position became more shaky, their treatment of civilian populations became more repressive.

One afternoon, as Frans and Dirk were starting home from school, they spotted Uncle Janus standing on a street corner. He had his hands thrust deep in his pockets and appeared not to have noticed the boys until they were standing right beside him. Then he pretended to shake Frans's hand, passing him a message as he did so, and he said, "Give this to your dad or to Dries." Then he turned abruptly and left.

The boys looked a bit flabbergasted, but Frans at once realized they had to act as if nothing had happened. He slipped the note into his pocket and the boys started for home again.

"What does it say?" asked Dirk excitedly.

Frans merely shrugged his shoulders. "I don't know."

"Why don't you look?" Dirk urged. "It must be something

special, otherwise Uncle Janus wouldn't act so mysterious."

Frans was curious too. But should he read the note? It was probably nothing; there wasn't even an envelope. It was just a piece of paper, folded once and closed with a piece of tape. In fact, he could probably read it without even removing the tape. If he wasn't allowed to read it, wouldn't Van Beveren have put it in an envelope or said something?

"Open it," pleaded Dirk, who was overcome with curiosity.

Frans glanced up and down the street. There were quite a few people around. It just wasn't safe, he decided. "Not here. Maybe later," he replied tersely.

They started to walk again, more quickly than before. It was chilly and damp. They shivered. Was it only because of the cold or was it excitement about the mysterious message hidden deep in Frans's pocket?

When they came to the bridge across the Kanaaldijk, they felt much safer. Frans furtively looked around to make sure no one was watching, but he didn't see anybody. Then he pulled out the note. He pushed the two edges toward each other so that he could read the writing on the inside.

"Nothing special," he said, disappointed. "Uncle Janus only needs a board to fix a hole in his roof. That's all."

"Then why all the secrecy?" Dirk insisted. He had had his hopes fixed on some dangerous plot, and he felt a bit cheated.

Frans knitted his brow; he tried to figure it out. It wasn't the first time they had been asked to deliver so-called "innocent" messages to their father. Usually it was all about cabbages or the like, but by now Frans knew that the cabbages were really fugitives. At first he had thought that this note was about another cabbage, but he had never read a message like this before. There was more at stake than a simple board, you could be sure of that.

He shoved the note back into his pocket and hurriedly walked on. As they approached the mill, as usual Snip came charging to meet them, barking excitedly and, of course, inviting them to a play-fight. He always went a little crazy when his friends came home from school.

The lights in the lumbershed were still burning and the circular saw was screaming. They decided to go directly to the lumbershed, since Father and Dries were still there.

"Hi scholars!" Mulders greeted them cheerfully. "Learn anything today?"

"We had fun in science today, Dad; that's always worth something!" shouted Dirk. His boyish voice rang out above the noise of the circular saw.

"If you're such a whiz in science, can you tell me what is the most unfortunate animal in creation?" his father asked.

Dirk was suddenly on guard. He knew when his father was trying to put one over on him. He hesitated for a moment, then shrugged his shoulders.

"A centipede with corns!" laughed Mulders.

Frans handed his father the note. "From Uncle Janus, Dad."

Mr. Mulders opened the note and read it. Suddenly the laughter vanished from his face and he looked drawn and serious. Without comment, he passed the note to Dries. Dries read it and quickly tore it into shreds, saying, "It's come,

Dad." His voice was grave, too, and yet it betrayed a certain satisfaction.

Mulders nodded silently. "Yes, it's come." Then he turned to Frans and Dirk. "Boys, you better go see your mother. She's waiting for you; we'll be along in a minute."

The boys knew they were being sent away so they wouldn't hear what was said. They would have loved to hear what was going on, but their father gave them no hint, he just pointed to the door. Disappointed and still bubbling with curiosity, they walked to the house.

CHAPTER XIII

The Squad's Strategy

Upstairs in Van Beveren's big house was a small attic room. In the room seven people had gathered—six men and a woman. Besides Van Beveren and his wife, there were Dries, Arie, Egbert and two other men, one about forty years old with a tanned, weathered face and jet black hair, and the other a red-headed youth not much older than Dries. They were known only as Frank and Joop. All the guests had one thing in common: they had all received a secret message from Janus. After dark, they had stealthily made their way to the old, run-down house. Two of them had been admitted by the front door; the rest had come through the alley and the back door. All of them had taken extreme care not to be spotted by any of the spies and fifth columnists in German employ.

From the outside the old house looked deserted. The attic room could be reached only by a ladder. When everybody was safely inside, Van Beveren had pulled up the ladder and closed the trapdoor. The seven people were as safe as they could expect to be during wartime.

Mrs. Van Beveren, known to all as Aunt Helena, poured some blackish-brown liquid that passed as coffee. The small room was warm and cozy, but there was also tension in the air.

Uncle Janus opened the discussion. "Men, I think you know what this is all about. We need ration cards for the fugitives we're hiding. We've had so many over the last few weeks that we've lost count, but we can't do without a supply of ration cards any longer.

"We've got to close the gap between supply and demand, and the only way to do that is to rob a distribution center. I have a plan. That's what we're here to discuss."

Van Beveren reached into his pocket and pulled out a folded piece of paper. He unfolded it and placed it flat on the small table. It was the plans of a distribution center. All gathered round.

"Very nice," smiled Arie. Van Beveren nodded.

"Thanks to Frank. He used to be a draftsman. This past week he paid a visit to the local distribution center. He pretended to be a representative for some manufacturer or other, and he hung around the office for about an hour or so, absorbing every detail of the building. When he left, he knew exactly where the ration cards were kept and how we could best get our hands on them."

Frank only smiled, a little embarrassed by all the praise heaped on him. "Ah, it wasn't all that hard," he protested weakly. "The whole trick was not to look suspicious and to build a convincing case for my product. And since I'm a pretty good talker, there were no problems at all."

Van Beveren went back to the plans. He made some marks on the paper. "This is the front of the building, and here's the front door. But, as you see, it's right on a busy street. Even at night there's quite a bit of traffic, especially German army vehicles. Anyway, it would take too long to pick the lock. That's out of the question.

"Behind the building there's a fence which shouldn't give us too much trouble. That's the easiest way to get to the back of the building. The windows downstairs are barred but not the ones upstairs. There's a downspout on this corner. You can see Frank paid a lot of attention to detail. Somebody who knows how to climb should be able to reach this window here, sit on the sill, and remove a pane of glass with a glass cutter. He'll have to climb in, go downstairs and open the back door for the rest of us. Frank will be with us to show us where the stuff is. When it's all over, we'll go out the same way we came in."

"That's a piece of cake," chuckled Egbert.

Van Beveren looked at him doubtfully, then shrugged his shoulders. "Perhaps. But you never know. There are a couple of problems. In the first place, we have to get in and out without being seen. In the second place, the distribution center adjoins the mansion of the new mayor. He's a member of the N.S.B. I don't know him myself, but they say he's more fanatical than most Nazi sympathizers. He used to be a policeman, I'm told. If he smells a rat, he'll alert the Germans immediately. Before we know it we'll have a whole division down our necks."

"Ah, it won't be that bad." Egbert remained optimistic.

"Probably not, but we have to be careful and we'll have to leave lookouts at strategic places while we're inside the building. The whole operation has to be done quickly and quietly. The quicker we are, the smaller the risks. But for some of us this will be our first job. And we must not fail."

They all nodded their agreement. Then they worked out the details. Van Beveren showed them a set of break-in tools and some other paraphernalia they would need. Then he glanced at his watch.

"We'll leave in fifteen minutes. Mother, why don't you pour us one more cup."

Mrs. Van Beveren filled up their cups again. The atmosphere in the room was very tense. Dries was eager and yet anxious; proud and yet fearful.

He knew what was at stake. He knew that if they were caught during the robbery, they'd be shot without a trial. But they had to get ration cards for the fugitives, and he was willing to risk his life for the lives of others.

The time had come to leave. Van Beveren opened the trap-door and lowered the ladder. Mrs. Van Beveren embraced her husband and shook hands with the other men. She probably had the hardest role to play. She had to wait, without knowing what was going on. But she held up bravely, even now.

Downstairs, Van Beveren told the others to wait while he went through the back door to check out the neighborhood.

Soon he was back, relieved and anxious to go. "We're in luck, guys. It's very foggy out there. That'll make it a lot easier for us."

Crossing the courtyard, they left by the door in the brick wall and through the alleyway. Van Beveren locked the door and put the key in his pocket. "Turn left," he whispered. Dries looked at him questioningly; to the left was a dead end. But he didn't ask any questions.

They reached a spot where they were surrounded by nothing but brick walls, warehouses on either side of them and the wall dead ahead. But on their right some iron hooks jutted from the wall. Using these, Van Beveren climbed over the brick wall. The others quickly followed him.

On the other side of the wall was a narrow corridor—a fire route Van Beveren explained. They made their way through the fog and darkness without encountering anyone. Off in the distance they heard faint traffic noises along the main street. That had to be Germans, or else people with special permits, because it was already way past curfew, and that meant that nobody was allowed outside without a written permit.

The fire route led to a wide street. From here on travel would be trickier, because they were a lot more exposed, but the fog provided good cover. Before they left the fire route, they listened carefully and checked in every direction. Off in the distance they heard vague sounds, but nearby nothing stirred.

Van Beveren quickly delivered some last minute instructions. "Walk as quietly as possible. We must hear everything and yet not be heard ourselves. If you notice somebody coming, duck into a sidestreet or else into a doorway. We'll turn right here and then take the third street left. Stay right behind me and stick close together."

They tiptoed on, keeping their eyes and ears open for the unexpected, but the street was deserted and not a living thing moved outside. They had to be very careful not to trip and fall, however, because the streets were pitch black since street lighting was not allowed. The cold, damp fog chilled the men to the bone, but they realized that it reduced the danger of being spotted.

From a sidestreet off to their right came footsteps. "Duck," Van Beveren whispered urgently. They felt their way around a corner of a building and vanished into an alleyway just as the footsteps turned into the street where they had been just a moment before. They were the confident footsteps of a constable on patrol. The men seemed relatively safe, and everything would have gone just fine had it not been for the shrill scream of a black alley cat. Joop had stepped on its tail!

The footsteps abruptly stopped. The men crept back as far as possible in the dark corner of the alley and held their breath.

The constable took out his flashlight and shone it on the sidewalk directly in front of him. The light beam caught the cat which blinked its green eyes in the sudden brightness and hissed at this intrusion.

The constable snapped off the light and continued his patrol. Behind him in the alleyway, the little group of conspirators heaved a deep sigh.

They waited until the footsteps had faded in the distance. Then they went on: first straight, then left, then through a couple of alleyways, across a square . . . The men no longer knew where they were going, but trusted Van Beveren's judgment. At long last they found themselves in a quiet back street. They floated through the misty night like gray ghosts until they reached the high wooden fence behind the distribution center.

CHAPTER XIV

Caught Redhanded

So far so good. The fence was about two meters high and was topped by two strands of barbed wire. "That won't be easy," Dries observed.

But he was wrong. Van Beveren went straight to a door in the fence. He tried the handle but the door was locked. Quickly he took a key ring out of his pockets and moments later they were inside. Stealthily, they made their way through the dark yard. Van Beveren debated whether to lock the door again but finally he decided that was too dangerous. If something went wrong inside, they would need a quick exit and this would be it.

He felt the inside of the door and discovered a latch. Excellent; they could fix it so nobody could get in, but if they needed to get out this way, they would be able to open it quickly enough.

That settled, they went on. They had studied the floor plan thoroughly, so they knew exactly where to go. They reached the rear of the building and, groping in the dark, found the downspout.

Now came the tricky part: Dries had to climb the pipe and get into the building through one of the windows. He tested the pipe to make sure it was securely fastened to the wall. If the top was as solid as the bottom and if the pipe was securely fastened to the eaves, he would be all right. But suppose it collapsed.

"Ready?" Van Beveren whispered. "Here's the glass cutter. Stick it in your pocket and stay calm, don't rush."

Dries nodded, not realizing that Van Beveren couldn't see it. Van Beveren passed him the glass cutter and a penlight to light his way if necessary. Then he grabbed hold of the downspout and began to climb.

The downspout held and Dries slowly pulled himself up toward the sill. Dries was athletic, agile and determined, so he was good at this sort of thing. He had often performed similar feats but only to show off, never with this much at stake.

When he thought he was high enough, he groped along the brick wall, but, no, the sill had to be a little higher. He climbed a little higher until he found the sill. Now came the most difficult part. He had to pull himself onto the sill and sit with his back to the window.

Fortunately the sill was fairly wide. A metal rail had been fastened onto it, probably to hold a flower box. Clutching the rail, he pulled himself up and sat on the sill. Taking a short rest, he whispered down to his mates that he had made it.

"Well done!" replied Van Beveren. He had been busy himself in the meantime—soaping up a big towel to help remove the pane of glass.

Dries took out the glass cutter, taking hold of the iron rail, he half turned and pressed the cutter against the glass. He had done this kind of work before but never in this position. Without the iron rail, he didn't see how he could possibly have done it. He could hardly hear the glass cutter as it slid across the surface of the glass. In the darkness Dries couldn't see whether the glass had been completely cut, but he would find out soon enough.

"Pass me the towel," he whispered. Frank had fetched a long board from over by the fence and Van Beveren fastened the towel to one end of it. Then he reached it up to Dries. Carefully Dries pressed the soapy side of the towel against the piece of glass he had just cut. It took a long time; the towel had to be perfectly flat against the pane of glass, otherwise it would slip and fall inside.

He pushed against the towel. There was a muffled snap as the cut piece popped loose. It stuck to the soapy side of the towel and Dries lifted it through the hole and leaned it against the wall inside.

The tricky part was over; the rest would be a cinch. He climbed in without too much difficulty and found himself in pitch black surroundings. He could see nothing, so he took out his penlight and quickly searched the room for a door. It was straight across the room, but he had to be careful not to trip over the desks and chairs in the room.

Switching off the light, he headed for the door. Fortunately it wasn't locked. After closing it behind him, he snapped on the light again and discovered that he was in a corridor. Just off to his right was the staircase leading down. No problem so far.

Dries was beginning to feel confident. He was proud that Van Beveren had entrusted the first step of the action to him and that so far he had succeeded.

At the foot of the staircase was another corridor leading to the back door. The back door was locked with two large dead bolts; they would never have been able to break these from the outside.

"You've done very well so far," said Van Beveren, slapping Dries on the shoulder. "Now for your jobs. Dries, you go to the front lobby and stand guard there. Joop, you go back to the fence and keep watch there. Arie, Egbert and Frank will remove the ration cards. I'm going upstairs to look around. There may be something up there we can use. And remember: no noise! The mayor's house is right next door; there's only a thin wall between the buildings."

Dries and Joop weren't particularly happy with their assignments—just standing around looking. They wouldn't be able to see anything in this fog anyway. That wasn't what they had come for. But they didn't dare protest. Van Beveren was the leader, and he demanded unquestioning obedience. So they went to their posts. Dries, at least, had the satisfaction of knowing that they wouldn't have gotten in had it not been for him. Joop, however, felt a little like a fifth wheel. Unhappily he skulked out to take his position at the fence. The fog was still as dense as before, in fact, probably more so. It even seemed to muffle the traffic sounds they had heard earlier.

Frank, Arie and Egbert got busy in the large office where the ration cards were stored. Frank succeeded in opening a large cabinet with one of his skeleton keys. They didn't turn on any lights; that would have been foolhardy. Arie stood back with a flashlight as Egbert and Frank quickly filled the burlap bag with armloads of ration cards. They beamed with delight at the sight of all the cards. "All right! Look at that! Cards for clothing, bread, tobacco, and a general purpose category. That'll tide us over for a while."

They cleaned out the whole cabinet, except for a small money box. They didn't want to seem like criminals, and money wouldn't do them much good anyway. After cleaning out the cabinet, they rifled through a couple of desks, but that was fruitless. Just to be sure they didn't miss anything, Frank opened another wall cabinet but it was completely empty. "I think we've got it all," he whispered.

Suddenly the room was flooded with light. Blinded, the three men stared about in confusion! A voice barked, "Hands up, and hurry up about it!"

It was the Nazi mayor, dressed only in pajamas. One look was enough to tell them he meant business. In his right hand he held a pistol aimed directly at the three men. Dazedly they raised their arms. There was little else they could do; they were convinced the man wouldn't hesitate to shoot if they didn't obey immediately.

Frank wondered how in the world this could have happened. How could he have gotten into the building without being spotted by one of the sentries? Briefly he weighed his chances if he were to jump the man and knock the pistol out of his hand, but he put it out of his mind. He'd be dead before he took two steps.

Their only chance was for one of the others to jump the man from behind. Or had they already been put out of action? "Face the wall and keep those hands up!" snarled the mayor. His eyes were cold and his voice menacing. They had no choice but to obey.

Meanwhile, Janus Van Beveren was busy upstairs. There were three rooms, but his examination turned up nothing. He did take some seals and rubber stamps, because they might be useful later. The largest office belonged to the director of the distribution center. Van Beveren knew him to be a fanatical Nazi. His staff didn't like him but, of course, the director was protected by the mayor.

Janus suddenly got the urge to play a nasty trick on him. What would be the best way to put the director in his place? He suppressed the idea as quickly as it had come. This was no time for funny stuff.

The beam of the flashlight flitted over the wall and came to rest on a large portrait of Mussert, leader of the N.S.B. At least he could do something about that. He took down the portrait and was just about to leave the room when he heard a snarl coming from downstairs: "Hands up and be quick about it!"

His knees almost buckled under him; something had gone wrong. Noiselessly, he opened the door to the corridor and listened. He saw that the lights were on downstairs. For a few seconds he stood rooted to the floor listening closely to what was going on downstairs. He soon concluded that there was only one man, not a whole squad as he had originally feared. The man had probably caught the boys in the act.

He regretted not having taken any guns, but it was too late now. That wouldn't happen again, at least, not if they got another chance.

Still carrying the portrait, he gingerly tiptoed down the corridor and carefully made his way down the staircase.

Again the voice barked a command, ordering the men to face the wall and keep their hands up. Janus was sure it was the mayor, although he couldn't figure out how he had gotten in. In any case, the mayor didn't seem to know that there were more people in the building. That was to their advantage.

The door to the hallway was open and bright light fell into the hall. Slowly, Janus edged down the hall to the door. He was directly behind the mayor who was standing behind the boys waving the pistol. The man was just about to take a step forward toward his prisoners, when Van Beveren leaped into the room and brought the huge portrait down hard on the man's head. Crash! The glass broke, the portrait and the cardboard behind it were ripped to shreds but the sturdy frame pinned the mayor's arms to his sides.

As the mayor's arms were knocked down, he accidentally pulled the trigger, but the bullet ricocheted harmlessly off the wall. At the same time, Frank whirled and leaped at the mayor, twisting the pistol out of his hand.

Instantly, the roles were reversed: the mayor, as astonished as his three victims had been earlier, was suddenly disarmed. Arie and Egbert also turned around, and Arie turned on the flashlight as Van Beveren turned off the lights. However, it didn't take the mayor long to recover his nerve.

"You'll regret this, you . . . you bandits!" he fumed.

"Bandits we're not. We fight for queen and country, but

you're in league with the enemy," replied Frank calmly. "All right, now you face the wall, or I'll shoot you down on the spot. Come to think of it, that would suit us best."

Frank meant exactly what he said. The mayor had seen their faces and, though he didn't know them, he would undoubtedly recognize them if he saw them again. There would be no danger of that if they disposed of him now. But they just couldn't bring themselves to shoot him down simply to minimize their own risks.

The mayor sensed he had better keep his mouth shut. This was no time to antagonize them; his life depended on humoring them. Without further argument he walked to the wall. Van Beveren, who had left the portrait frame hanging around the man's shoulders, withdrew into the background. The mayor hadn't seen his face, and Janus was careful not to say a word.

"How did you know we were here?" Frank demanded.

All at once the mayor became very cooperative. They had just recently installed a new alarm system, he told his captors. Under the carpet in front of the cabinet where the ration cards were kept was an alarm. Anyone opening the cabinet door couldn't help tripping the alarm. During the day it was disengaged but at all other times it was turned on. The trigger was connected to an alarm bell in the mayor's house. When they had opened the ration card cabinet, they had stepped on the trigger, tipping off the mayor.

"How did you get here?" Frank wanted to know. The mayor told him. In the next room was a large walk-in cabinet. The back of the cabinet was covered with a curtain but behind the curtain was a secret door. It had been installed only recently. Since the door led to his house, the mayor was the only one who had a key.

Frank had to admit it wasn't a bad idea. There was something of the old policeman still left in the mayor. Apparently it had been his idea to install the alarm system, so he had to be given credit for having brains. And he wasn't afraid either, otherwise he wouldn't have tackled them singlehandedly.

Van Beveren was becoming impatient. The fact that the mayor was suddenly so cooperative and talkative made him uneasy. Only, he had no idea why. But somehow he had the feeling that their clever antagonist would get the better of them yet. It was time to vanish, he decided, but first they would have to make sure he couldn't raise the alarm.

CHAPTER XV

A Narrow Escape

Dries was still at the front door. He had experienced a few anxious moments. When he had suddenly heard the strange, snarling voice, he had realized something was wrong. Very carefully opening the door to the hallway, he saw that the lights were on. As he was debating what to do, he saw Van Beveren approach from the other side. Shortly thereafter he had heard a shot, but he had quickly learned that his friends had turned the tables on their enemy. He wanted to go and find out more, but he was reminded of Van Beveren's order not to leave his post. If they needed him, they would call on him.

So, still nervous, he sauntered to the other side of the lobby. He doubted whether his being here did any good, because he couldn't see anything anyway. It was more a question of using his ears than his eyes. But all was quiet outside. The only sounds he picked up were those coming from the room where his friends were. One voice was doing most of the talking, and it sounded like he was trying to explain something.

Wait, what was that? He heard a noise outside. It was the muffled whine of an engine rapidly coming closer. It had to be a car or a truck. Dries tuned out the sounds coming from inside and listened only to the engine sound. The vehicle would probably barrel right on by, but you could never know . . .

Off to the right, just beyond the mayor's house, was a street corner. Suddenly Dries saw dim lights penetrating the fog. They were masked headlights—headlights that had been blacked out except for a small slit in the center. Although Dries couldn't see the vehicle, the position of the headlights convinced him that it was a large German military van. It stopped at the street corner.

Then Dries heard the sound of soldiers jumping down out of the van. Hobnail boots clattered on the pavement; the soldiers were running straight to the distribution center. Others veered off into a sidestreet.

Dries dashed down the hall, shouting, "Get out; the Germans are coming!"

That triggered a near panic. Only the mayor was relaxed and satisfied, smug even.

Van Beveren could have kicked himself. How could he have been so dumb! The mayor had almost certainly called the Germans and alerted them to what was going on. Then he had gone out on his own, thinking to get the credit for capturing them himself. But he had known that the German soldiers would be right behind him. That's why he had been so talkative. He was buying time, enough time for the Germans to get here from their barracks.

This realization was instantaneous as was his reaction. He sprang forward, pushed the gloating mayor into a closet, and quickly locked the door. Egbert seized the burlap bag with ration cards and they all charged for the door. Halfway to the back door they ran into Joop, who blurted, "There's a whole squad of Germans at the fence! They're breaking down the door!"

In the lobby where Dries had stood guard a window was smashed. Apparently the Germans were already there.

"Come on; there's only one way out," hissed Janus. He ran to the wall closet by which the mayor had entered, threw open the doors and drew the curtain aside. There was the door to the mayor's house, and the key was still in the lock.

It took them about two seconds to get through the door and close it behind them. Van Beveren had enough presence of mind to take out the key and lock the door on the inside. As it clicked shut, they could hear the first of the Germans running through the long corridor.

On the other side of the partition was an identical wall cabinet which brought them into the mayor's house. They raced to the front door, which was on the side of the house facing away from the distribution center.

Van Beveren opened it a little and peeked out. The fog was less dense than before. As far as Van Beveren could tell, there were no Germans on this side of the building. But their escape route would soon be discovered. Van Beveren's mind was churning; with his plans for an orderly withdrawal shot to pieces, he had to devise a new escape route.

He saw the German military van parked on the street corner and it gave him an idea. Carefully he opened the door all the way and they slipped outside. Out on the porch, Van Beveren whispered new instructions. "There's the German van. We'll commandeer it to make our escape. Frank and I will jump in the front, the rest of you in the back. If it doesn't start, we'll leg it down the sidestreet. There's still enough fog to give us cover. Shoes off and let's go!"

A second later, they were all charging toward the van. Frank was carrying the Luger in his hand. They might have to shoot their way into the van. Well, war was war.

But there was no one with the van, and the key was still in the ignition.

"All right, climb in and let's go!"

Arie, Egbert, Dries and Joop tumbled in over the tailgate while Janus and Frank leaped into the front seat. Van

Beveren started the engine.

As the engine roared into life, two German soldiers who had been posted at the front door of the distribution center shouted angrily. Two shots rang out almost simultaneously, then a third, but they were off target. The van lurched away and shot down the sidestreet.

Its six occupants hooted with joy. They had gotten away, they still had the loot, and, in addition, they had picked up a getaway car.

Van Beveren stepped down on the accelerator. This was dangerous in the foggy, unlit streets, but Van Beveren was an expert driver and he knew every street around here. He just assumed that all the streets would be deserted. He didn't have much choice; they had to make their getaway quickly and put some distance between themselves and the Germans before they could set up roadblocks.

As they drove, they discussed the emergency plan. Frank, Arie and Egbert would have to vanish from the area. The other three were relatively safe because the mayor hadn't seen their faces. They could go back to their own homes, even though they would have to be very careful.

Somewhere behind them a siren broke the stillness of the night. The Germans had started in pursuit.

Van Beveren pushed down the accelerator even farther. The van clattered onto the bridge across the canal, then turned left onto the Kanaaldijk. Minutes later the van stopped in front of the mill. Van Beveren, Dries and Joop jumped out with the loot as Frank slid behind the steering wheel. Arie and Egbert joined him in the front.

Van Beveren gave them some final instructions how to drive and where to hide out. They would have to get rid of the German military vehicle as soon as they could.

"Right!" replied Frank as he started the engine and drove off into the fog and darkness.

The three others walked to the house. Just as they got

there, Mulders came out. He and his wife had stayed up all night worrying about Dries. The threesome received a royal welcome. They were led inside, served hot milk, and Mr. Mulders fired up the stove.

Van Beveren told them what had happened. It was better, he thought, to tell Mulders and his wife everything, because then they could help plan what to do next.

Van Beveren's greatest concern was for Frank, Arie and Egbert. If they were picked up, they were dead. But Van Beveren assured him that they were clever young men, who had been in situations like this before.

Mulders offered to hide the ration cards until it was safe to pick them up. Van Beveren and Joop decided to spend the night here. Mulders promised to awaken them early the next morning and row them to the other side of the canal, so they could steal back into the city undetected.

Dries went to bed. His head was whirling. He wouldn't soon forget the fear and suspense. He was immensely grateful to be alive. Before he went to sleep he knelt beside his bed and thanked God for saving them.

When he woke up the next morning, Frans and Dirk had already gone to school. The events of the previous night now seemed like a dream to him. There was only the fog to remind him of what had really happened.

Van Beveren and Joop had left earlier. None of them knew what had happened to them or to the three young men who had gone on in the German truck.

Dries gulped down a sandwich and then went to the shed to help his father. But his mind wasn't on his work. Neither, for that matter, was his father's.

After half an hour Mulders gave up. "Why don't you clean up around here," he said. "I'm going to town to run some errands and see what I can find out."

Dries stayed behind with his anxiety. He wanted to go to town himself, but his father wouldn't let him.

Mulders returned just before lunch, and his face showed unmistakable relief. He had talked to several people. The whole city seemed to know about the raid and the mayor's involvement. The story had captured the people's imagination, and the more the story was told the more it was glamorized.

Mulders had innocently asked around who had carried out the raid, but nobody seemed to know.

But what did the Germans know? Mulders had even strolled in the direction of the distribution center. Several Dutch police officers were walking about, but also some uniformed Germans. The Germans had looked furious. That, Mr. Mulders concluded, was a hopeful sign.

Toward evening he went to town again. He returned with the latest edition of the local paper, one that willingly printed all German propaganda. It carried a long-winded account of the break-in and the heroic efforts of the mayor to stop it single-handedly. But the "bandits" had finally managed to overpower the hero.

Nothing was said about the intervention of the German army or about the stolen German army vehicle. That was to be expected; the Germans would have been a laughingstock.

The paper went on to assure its readers that the "bandits" would soon be caught, but Mulders felt that this was only a bluff; it looked more like the Germans had no leads.

Two days later Van Beveren picked up the ration cards, which made Mulders very happy. He had found a good hiding place for them but it always remained a risky business, particularly because he felt sure that the Germans or their henchmen were always keeping an eye on the mill. Two days after the raid two Guardsmen had shown up, ostensibly to inquire after the price of wood. Mulders had gotten rid of them as fast as he could, because he had sensed that they had only come to snoop around.

For the first few days after the successful raid, Dries had been very tense. The Germans would undoubtedly do everything in their power to find the culprits, and the mayor, a former policeman himself, would throw all his weight behind the investigation.

But a week later Van Beveren let him know that Frank, Arie and Egbert had reached safety. That was a tremendous relief to Dries. Gradually the event slipped out of the public's mind. Raids were happening all over the place, sometimes with stunning success. The Resistance concentrated on obtaining ration cards and official papers. During one raid on a city hall in a big city the Resistance bagged 105,000 identity cards. This would help large numbers of fugitives; it gave thousands new names and a new lease on life.

Talk of liberation was beginning to make the rounds again too. Radio Orange, the Dutch station in England, began to send out instructions telling the people what to do in the event of an Allied invasion.

The pressure was making the Germans nervous. They began to make announcements in the papers that the low-lying parts of the Netherlands would be flooded if the Allies tried to invade here.

The Nazi oppression grew worse and worse. People were picked up indiscriminately. More men and women were being executed because they continued to champion the right to freedom for their nation and their people. Every day, tens of thousands of people pleaded to God for deliverance.

CHAPTER XVI

Trapped!

The raid gave Van Beveren and his squad their first taste of action. This was especially true of Dries, who fervently hoped that something else would happen soon. Van Beveren was of the same mind, of course, but he was experienced enough to know that you couldn't rush these things. Of the original six, only he, Dries and Joop were left. The other three were safe and sound, but they could no longer operate in this vicinity. So the whole squad had to be reorganized. That had to be done carefully, painstakingly, because one wrong choice could have disastrous results for the whole Resistance movement.

Besides, Janus had to arm the squad in case they had to defend themselves. This took a lot of time too. And the squad wasn't the only work he was involved in. There was always the recurring problem of fugitives who needed either temporary or permanent hiding places.

A few more were housed in the mill. Mulders realized it was dangerous, but he couldn't see how he could refuse shelter to people who were on the run. They usually stayed for only a short time, but as soon as they left, their places were taken by new ones.

As couriers, Frans and Dirk became very busy. Usually they went to Van Beveren's house to pick up messages, but often Van Beveren would be waiting for them somewhere on a street corner. He would often give them each an apple, but he would also secretly give them a note to take home. Usually it was the same old message having to do with cabbages.

The boys often thought back to Jaap Roseboom, the Jewish boy who had been with them during Christmas vacation. Once Frans had asked Uncle Janus how Jaap was doing. He had simply replied, "As far as I know he's okay." He hadn't elaborated, either because he didn't know or didn't want to tell.

Late winter brought chilly, gusty days with a lot of rain and wet snow. Each day anew the boys had to brace the miserable weather, and their clothes were in very poor condition. But there was little chance of getting anything new. Their mother did whatever sewing and patching she could, but it wasn't enough to keep Frans and Dirk from shivering on their way back and forth to school. Even impulsive, carefree Dirk was becoming downright zealous where his clothes were concerned. His mother had warned him repeatedly to take care of his clothes; otherwise he would have to go to school in rags.

One day the boys came home with a message that made Dries very happy. It was just like all the other times: a very innocent little message, but it told Dries that Van Beveren had finished reorganizing the squad and that he had also obtained the necessary weapons. He was told to report to a warehouse just outside the city that Saturday afternoon.

Dries was familiar with the factory, although it was at the other end of town. He thought it a very peculiar place to hold a meeting. There were many other factories around there, one of which was watched by the Germans night and day, because it was a munitions and weapons factory. Furthermore, about a kilometer down the road were German anti-aircraft installations. Why, he wondered, had Van Beveren elected to hold a meeting right in the middle of the spider's web? His father also read the note. Yes, that's what it said, however cryptic the message might be. Mr. Mulders didn't like it at all. He feared for Dries's life. But he had earlier given his approval, and he couldn't very well back out now.

That Saturday afternoon Dries left early. He had promised his folks that he would be very careful, and he meant it, although he wasn't nearly as worried as his father. If Van Beveren thought it was all right to meet in the factory, why should he question it?

The weather was good. For once, the sun shone, but it was one of those unconvincing, watery, winter suns. But the wind was less bothersome than it had been for the last few days. Whistling happily, he cycled through the town. He rode past the mayor's house and the distribution center and grinned at the memories of that evening.

He rode through the center of town and out into the country again. In the distance he spotted the factory. Everything was deserted, and there was no sign of danger.

Gradually Dries slowed down, and attentively studied the surroundings. The pale sun had disappeared behind a cloud and the countryside looked suddenly gray and menacing. The water in the canal, too, looked dark and leaden and ominous. Everything around him seemed somber and threatening. To his left were some bare, dreary trees and that didn't help his spirits at all. Dries got the irrational feeling that he was being spied upon by a thousand eyes.

"Ah," he scolded himself. "Nonsense! Don't let your imagination get the best of you." He speeded up again. The factory warehouse was dead ahead and, less than two hundred meters further, the munitions and weapons factory. At least Van Beveren hadn't decided to meet there!

He entered the yard, parked his bicycle and walked along the side of the building. There were several doors there and he tried them all, but only the last one was unlocked. All the while he wondered what he would say if he were confronted by a stranger. He opened the last door and walked into the cafeteria.

Van Beveren was sitting by a little table on which lay a briefcase bulging with papers. He smiled and extended his hand. "You're right on time! It'll be a while before the others get here."

Dries glanced around. "Is Joop here?"

Van Beveren shook his head. "He came down with the flu. He's sorry he couldn't come, but he has to sweat it out first."

"Who are the new members?"

"Three strong, experienced men. Their names are Henk, Fred and Barteld. That's all we know. They don't live here in the city, but they're not too far out. Headquarters has assigned them to our squad. Originally I only asked for weapons because I wanted to pick my own men, but headquarters insisted we take these three.

"I had a long talk with them, and they made a good impression on me. They're going to work out just fine."

"How will they get here if they don't live here?" asked Dries.

"You'll have to see for yourself! Anyway, they're coming by car. That surprises you, doesn't it. It's an old Ford but it's in excellent condition. More importantly: they all have their proper papers, licenses and permits to drive a car and buy gasoline. They're all phony of course, but that doesn't matter. They should be here in about fifteen minutes. They're also bringing weapons."

Dries was quickly developing a lot of respect for the three newcomers. They had to be very clever; otherwise Van Beveren wouldn't be as generous with his praise. Dries wanted to know more, but he stifled his curiosity. Too many questions was no good in this kind of business.

"Quite a briefcase," he observed, pointing at the table.

Van Beveren nodded. All at once Dries saw that the old man's face looked drawn and worried. "That's for Fred. It contains the addresses of hundreds of fugitives and a lot more secret information. I've had these things in my possession for months now, and I've also been responsible for supplying ration cards for these people, but the Germans are closing in. I'm not too worried about myself, but if this stuff were to fall into the wrong hands, it would be catastrophic."

"Do they know about this?" asked Dries, clearly startled.

"They don't exactly know anything, but they've got their suspicions. You remember that guy Dreumel, the one who barged into my backyard. He's never forgiven me for that. He keeps poking around my place, and apparently he's discovered something. He had relayed the information to the police. Fortunately I know somebody inside the police force, who tipped me off the day before yesterday. During the next day or two they'll search my place, and the Germans will demolish the whole house, if necessary, to find any secret papers. When I heard that, I had to get them out as quickly as possible."

"But what about you and Aunt Helena? You'll be arrested!"

Van Beveren merely shrugged his shoulders. "Maybe. I've thought about going into hiding with my wife, but I think I'll wait and see first. All the incriminating evidence is out of my house now. If they find nothing, who knows, maybe they'll let us go."

Dries wasn't at all sure, but he sensed from the look on his friend's face that he didn't want to discuss his own safety. So he kept quiet, but unhappily so. Talking could be just as dangerous as knowing too much. There were many kinds of secrets in the Resistance movement. Janus had already mentioned "headquarters" and the fact that there were hundreds of fugitives. Those were things Dries had suspected, but he hadn't really known for sure. Moreover, he didn't want to be inquisitive. He only asked why they were meeting in this factory cafeteria.

"You probably think it's risky so close to the Germans," laughed Van Beveren. "But don't worry. A good friend of mine is a guard here and he gave me the key. He told me that nobody ever comes here on Saturdays. And as far as the Germans are concerned, well, the fact that they're practically next door is our insurance that nobody will interfere. Who's going to expect the Resistance to hold a meeting here? In any event, we had to meet somewhere, and this place seemed the most suitable. My house isn't safe under the circumstances and neither is your mill.

"At first I considered leaving you out of it, but finally I decided to include you anyway. If I get picked up, you'll have to become the contact for Henk, Fred and Barteld. So you have to get acquainted. This afternoon's meeting will be short; we'll just discuss a couple of essential things. We'll meet again sometime soon to plan a course of action."

Janus walked to the window and looked out. "They're

late," he observed. He tried to sound casual, but there was a trace of worry in his voice.

Dries was becoming restless. He paced up and down and tried to calm his nerves. After a while he strolled to the door connecting the cafeteria with the workshop. "Mind if I look around?" he asked.

"Go ahead. I'll call you when they show up," replied Van Beveren.

Dries shut the door behind him and wandered about in the workshop. There were all kinds of tool making machinery here. Dries soon became absorbed in the equipment and forgot his anxiety as he tried to figure out what everything was for.

He had reached the far end of the workshop when he heard voices coming from the cafeteria. That had to be the three new men, Dries decided. But the voices sounded loud and angry. Dries shrugged it off and quickly walked back. Just as he was about to open the door, however, he heard somebody turn over a table and shout, "Leave that briefcase alone, you Bolshevik, and put up your hands or I'll put a bullet between your eyes!"

Dries froze. He immediately realized what had happened: the enemy had gotten wind of the meeting. For a few seconds he just stood and listened to what was going on. There were more voices, at least three or four more. It didn't sound like Van Beveren was resisting.

What should he do? Barge inside? He looked around, picked up a heavy adjustable wrench but put it down again. No, force wasn't the answer, he decided, but he couldn't leave Janus in the lurch either.

The door had a latch. Gingerly, he slid it in place. At least they wouldn't be able to get at him. He bent down and peeked through the keyhole. Van Beveren was standing with his back against the wall. His face was a mask, but his eyes were filled with despair.

There were five other men in the room, and one of them was Dreumel. He had a gun in his hand and was pointing it straight at Janus. The other four were Guardsmen armed with shotguns. One of them was holding the briefcase.

Dries trembled violently—with terror but also with anger. He had to help Janus! But how?

Feverishly his brain cast around for a solution. Then it occurred to him; he turned away from the door and tiptoed through the workshop toward the far end.

CHAPTER XVII

When All Is Lost, Bluff...

Reaching the far end, he opened a window, climbed out and ran to his bike. He was lucky that the men in the cafeteria couldn't see him from there. At least, not as long as they stayed inside. If they decided to take their prisoner outside, they would spot him right away. He had to be quick.

Jumping on his bike, he raced toward the road, turning in the direction of the city. The thought flitted through his mind that his hurried flight might attract the attention of the German soldiers next door. But he couldn't do anything about that; he had to risk it.

For the first few seconds he fully expected to hear a shot ring out behind him, but nothing happened, and he was quickly putting more distance between himself and the factory. He had made it!

But he wasn't just concerned about himself; he had to rescue Janus. He knew that Henk, Fred and Barteld could arrive at any moment. Somehow he had to intercept them and tell them what had happened. Together they might be able to find some way to spring Janus.

But how? Never mind; they had to! He couldn't leave his old friend to fend for himself. What was keeping those new men? It was an old Ford, Janus had said. Well, he couldn't very well miss that. He was getting close to the city. If he went into town, however, he might miss the car. What was keeping them? There was no telling what those thugs might be doing to Janus.

He halted just outside the city limits. He decided the best thing to do was to wait. But waiting wasn't easy under the circumstances. Dries looked about anxiously, one way to see if the old Ford was coming, and the other to see if Dreumel and his associates had left the factory. Once Janus was turned over to the Germans, they might as well give him up for lost.

Minutes ticked by and nothing happened. Dries's nerves were getting the best of him. Then he heard the growl of an engine coming closer. It came from the city. Suddenly, an old car came from between the houses and turned onto the Kanaaldijk in the direction of the factory.

Dries never doubted that this was the car. He stepped out onto the street and held up his hand, but the driver showed no sign of slowing down. "Stop! Stop!" yelled Dries, but without result; the car came straight at him. At the last second, he jumped aside. He had to leave his bike and a split second later it was crumpled under the left front wheel of the car.

The driver slowed down but he still didn't stop. As the car passed, Dries grabbed the door on the driver's side and jumped onto the running board.

Finally the car came to a standstill; the driver opened the door and shouted angrily, "What's the matter with you, kid? Are you trying to get yourself killed?"

Dries ignored the outburst. Still panting, he said, "I—I wanted to warn you. They got Janus . . ."

All at once the three men sat up, but they weren't wholly convinced. Three pairs of eyes stared suspiciously at Dries.

"Janus? We don't know any Janus," barked the driver.

Dries felt the sweat breaking out all over. Had he stopped

the wrong car? Of course, they were just playing it safe.

"I mean Janus Van Beveren! My name is Dries Mulders and you're Henk, Fred and Barteld. We were waiting for you, and Van Beveren was surprised by five men, Guardsmen and members of the N.S.B. They grabbed him and his briefcase with the addresses of the fugitives."

The three men in the car no longer doubted him. They knew, from his words and his obvious anxiety, that he was telling the truth. One of them jumped out and pulled the twisted bicycle out from under the car. "There. Too bad about that bicycle. We didn't want to stop because we were afraid it was an ambush. But come on, get in and tell us exactly what happened."

Dries got in, the doors were slammed shut, and the driver pulled the car up a few meters and parked it on the shoulder.

The boy gave a quick account of events at the factory. His audience listened attentively. Janus's arrest was bad enough in itself, but if the Germans got a hold of all the secret papers it would be a disaster.

"Are they still there?" asked Fred, who seemed to be the leader.

Dries hesitated. "I think so. In any case, they didn't come back this way, so they're probably still there."

Fred was noticeably relieved. "Then we'll see if we can spring him. We've got weapons and if necessary we'll shoot our way in."

Dries shook his head glumly. "You can't do that. There's a munitions and weapons factory right next door and there are dozens of German soldiers there. Besides, there are anti-aircraft batteries on the other side. As soon as we start shooting, we're finished."

Fred looked crestfallen. This wasn't going to be easy. They held a hurried council of war. There wasn't a moment to lose.

"There's only one way," concluded Fred. "They've probably already called the Germans. We could expect a van along here any second to pick up Van Beveren. We have to beat them to it. If we pose as members of the Gestapo, they might release him to us."

The others nodded their approval. It was a good idea, but actually something that required a lot more preparation. But that was out of the question. There was no time. They had to gamble.

"Is there a telephone booth around here?" Fred asked.

Dries nodded. "Two blocks back in town at the second street corner."

"Beautiful. Henk, you're our German expert. You call up the factory and tell them we're coming to pick up the terrorist they've arrested."

They wheeled the car around and quickly drove back. As they stopped at the telephone booth, Henk and Dries jumped out. Dries rifled through the telephone book and found the factory's number. Henk lifted the receiver and dialed the number.

"Hello!" Dreumel answered the phone.

Henk began speaking in perfect German. Although Dries couldn't follow everything that he said, he was startled at the sudden transformation in Henk. His voice was hard and clipped and even the expression on his face was very different, very arrogant.

The discussion didn't last long. Henk asked a few questions and barked out a few orders and that was the end of it. Dries hadn't understood half of it.

Henk hung up and immediately changed back to his former self. He beamed and said, "We stand a pretty good chance. Come on, let's go!"

They dashed back to the car, which had turned around in the meantime, and jumped in. Barteld sped off. When they were moving Henk told them the gist of the conversation.

"That guy"—it was Dreumel, Dries explained—"was surprised at first. It seems they've been trying to pump Van Beveren on their own and were just about to call the Gestapo when my call came in. I pretended I was a member of the S.D. When Dreumel asked how we knew they were there, I snarled at him that nothing escapes the notice of the S.D. and that some of the German soldiers next door had alerted us. When I complimented him and his mates on the good job they had done, they were tickled pink. I told him we'd be right over to pick up the terrorist and that they should stay there until we got there. So our chances look pretty good—unless they see through the whole scheme at the last minute."

"If they do we'll open up," Fred said simply. "But I think we can bluff them."

Barteld had remained silent. He needed all his attention for his driving; he had the accelerator pressed to the floor.

Fred, who was sitting in the back, produced three pistols and three armbands with swastikas on them. Sliding one armband onto his sleeve and putting one pistol in his pocket, he handed the others around.

They were very close to the factory yard and also to the

munitions factory. Dries's heart raced in suspense.

Fred nudged him. "Do you drive?" he asked.

Dries nodded.

"Good. You stay in the car and get behind the steering wheel. We'll leave the engine running. The minute we get back in the car, step on it. We don't want to hang around here any longer than necessary."

Barteld swung the car onto the yard and turned it so that it was facing the road. The three men jumped out. Dries slid behind the steering wheel, careful to remain hidden from view.

Fred and his comrades marched to the door, yanked it open and quickly marched inside.

Van Beveren still sat with his back against the wall. His wrinkled face was marked with welts and bruises. His tormentors were sitting around him in a semi-circle. The moment the three "Germans" marched in, they jumped up and thrust out their right arms.

Fred and his men returned the salute. Immediately Henk started yelling orders in a harsh, strident voice. He upbraided the "terrorist" and loudly praised the virtues of the N.S.B. party faithful. The Guardsmen's faces lit up with childlike pride.

For a moment Van Beveren had blinked, but then his face was expressionless again.

Fred walked up to him and started slapping him around. He made sure it looked and sounded a lot worse than it was, but it could hardly be called gentle. He had to convince the others that they were S.D. officers and that they were venting their anger on this terrorist.

Aside from a few blows that were a little more realistic than he might have liked, Janus didn't mind. Never before had he suffered a beating with so much relief and pleasure.

Abruptly the three S.D. officers cut it short. There was a lot at stake, and their little charade might be discovered at any moment. "We're taking the terrorist and his papers with us," Henk barked suddenly and he snatched the briefcase from the table. Suddenly something occurred to him. He turned to Dreumel and ordered, "You men keep watch here the rest of this afternoon. There will probably be more Resistance people coming here. Make sure none of them get away. You've done very nicely so far, but I'm not satisfied."

It all sounded very convincing, but for a moment Henk wondered whether it would really work.

It did. The Nazi lackeys had been greatly flattered by the praise he had heaped on them. They promised to stay until deep into the night.

Fred shoved Van Beveren to the door. He leveled his pistol at him and warned him he would shoot if he made one wrong move. Henk followed, carrying the briefcase under his arm. Barteld, who had remained aloof as if guarding the door, closed ranks behind them.

A few more steps and they would be outside. Suddenly Dreumel stirred. He said, with a hint of suspicion in his voice, "Ah, may we see your papers, gentlemen?"

"Ach, jawohl, natürlich," replied Henk casually, but his heartbeat was far from casual. He had lots of German papers on him complete with official stamps and signatures, but if these men decided to take a close look, they would see that they weren't the right ones. Henk whipped out his wallet, opened it quickly and flashed about a dozen or so very official looking German papers in front of Dreumel's face. Then he decisively snapped it shut.

Dreumel, who had had only a hint of suspicion to start with, nodded respectfully. He hadn't had a chance to inspect the papers, but all those official stamps together with the speed with which the Gestapo acceded to his request had erased the last remaining doubt.

Fred and his men snapped to attention and saluted smartly. The Guardsmen, a little off balance, did the same. It had all been very impressive. The showdown had all been very one-sided and Dreumel really never had a chance.

Thirty seconds later they were climbing into the car as Dries waited in a cold sweat. He stepped on the gas and the car lurched across the yard and out onto the street. For the first little while nobody said a word; first they had to get out of there.

Half a kilometer down the road, Dries stopped the car and invited Barteld to take over. Barteld, he knew, was a much better driver. There was no sign of pursuit. The rescue had gone off without a hitch. Suddenly they all began talking at the same time.

"Did they give you a rough time?" Fred asked Van Beveren.

"Well, it wasn't a picnic," he admitted. "They had a lot of frustrations to work off. Naturally Dreumel wanted to get even. They wanted to squeeze the information out of me themselves so they could impress the Germans. Idiots! The most important information was in that briefcase, but they hadn't even looked in it when you came in. Boy, was I ever glad to see you! My life wouldn't have been worth a plugged nickle if they had turned me over to the Germans. Thanks very much!"

"Don't mention it; you'd have done the same for us," replied Fred. "Dries intercepted and warned us. First we wanted to gun down those traitors, but that was too dangerous because of the Germans next door. So we had to think of something else. But you'll have to go underground, together with your wife."

Van Beveren nodded. "I'm glad to get the chance. We've been getting ready for this. My wife has packed some suit-cases already, knowing it would come sooner or later. Let's go to the house and pick her up. Henk, it was clever of you to tell those guys to stay there until evening. Now at least they can't tip off the Germans."

"Not unless they get impatient and reach for the telephone," replied Henk.

Until now Barteld hadn't said a word. He had been paying attention to his driving, but had been listening to the conversation just the same. Now a broad grin came to his face. "They won't call, not unless they find the loose wire."

The others looked at him, puzzled. Barteld sat behind the steering wheel shaking with laughter.

"When Fred and Henk were busy with Van Beveren and those other good-for-nothings, I checked around to see where the telephone wire was. It ran behind a cabinet against the wall. I took out my wire cutters and reached behind the cabinet and cut the wire. They can try to call all they like; they won't get far."

"Excellent!" chuckled Fred. "That may give us a couple of extra hours. Still, we better hurry."

Sobering up, Barteld pressed the accelerator to the floor again. Van Beveren told him where to go.

For his own safety, they dropped Dries off before they reached Van Beveren's house. Janus shook Dries's hand and complimented him for the way he had handled the crisis. Fred promised that he would stay in touch with Dries. Together they would rebuild the squad, because the struggle was far from over.

Dries had to walk; his bicycle was wrecked. But he had no regrets. He had narrowly escaped with his life and had helped rescue his friend. He felt very grateful; the Lord had looked after them again.

The men drove straight to Van Beveren's neighborhood. They stopped at the alley that led to Van Beveren's backyard. Van Beveren jumped out but his friends stayed in the car.

It didn't take long. Less than fifteen minutes later Van Beveren and his wife emerged from the alley and climbed into the car. All they had with them was a couple of suitcases and a few other small items.

Mrs. Van Beveren's eyes were red, but she had composed herself again. Smiling, she sat back as the car roared off through the city streets toward the open country. Uncle Janus and Aunt Helena, who had found shelter for so many fugitives, had in turn become fugitives. Even as they were leaving, Van Beveren was already wondering how he might rise from the ashes and resume the fight for his country.

CHAPTER XVIII

Darkness before the Dawn

One evening, three days later, the whole Mulders family was sitting around the family table. The coal oil lamp was lit and the windows had been securely blacked out.

It was a stormy night. The wind had picked up late that afternoon and it still seemed to be increasing. Mother glanced anxiously at the woodstove; it was only woodscraps they were burning, and with this wind there was a tremendous draft, so the wood burned like paper.

Frans and Dirk were still up and were engrossed in a game of checkers. As usual, Dirk was doing most of the talking. He could easily have won this game, he claimed, if only Frans hadn't fouled him up.

Father was sunk deep in thought. Dries was reading a book, or pretending to, but his thoughts were elsewhere. Nel was busy writing a letter, and Mother, as usual, was repairing boys' clothes.

Two days ago Frans and Dirk had come home with the story that the Germans had completely gutted Van Beveren's home. Their father had assured them that Van Beveren was long gone. The boys weren't sure exactly what had happened. Dries had told only his father and mother about the incident

at the factory. Mulders and his wife had been badly
frightened by the story. Naturally they admired their son's
courage and presence of mind, but they also shuddered at the
thought that he could easily have been killed.

Dries had also told them that Fred would probably pick
him up someday soon to continue the work Van Beveren had
begun. His father had been very glum because he realized the
immense danger Dries would be exposed to. But again he
didn't have the heart to order Dries to stop.

That afternoon Mr. Mulders had been to town and had
learned, from a couple of trustworthy friends, that Mr. and
Mrs. Van Beveren were safe. But he had also learned that
German reprisals were becoming more severe; everywhere,
Dutch people were being arrested, sentenced to death, and
executed. The Germans and their Dutch lackeys were becoming
more ruthless by the day.

Mulders glanced at his son. Dries sensed his father's glance
on him and looked up. He tried to smile, but it was forced.
Dries knew what was bothering his father. He realized that he
would have to risk his life again and again, and yet he had no
second thoughts. It was work that had to be done.

Frans and Dirk were sent to bed. They hugged their father
and mother and went upstairs. Nel poured a cup of imitation
coffee for the others.

High above the anguished wail of the wind came a new
sound: the steady drone of airplane engines. By now that
sound was commonplace; they were English or American
bombers enroute to their targets in Germany. Presently, the
wail and drones were punctuated by the heavy, thudding
sound of anti-aircraft fire.

Mulders couldn't stand it any longer. Abruptly he got up to
go outside.

"You sure you want to do that?" asked his wife nervously.

Mulders replied reassuringly, "There's no danger. The
bombers are at the other end of the city."

"Can I come with you, Dad?" Dries asked. His father only nodded.

The fierce wind almost snatched away their breath. Quickly they walked to the giant silhouette of the mill—a lonely sentinel and a beacon of hope for so many fugitives. Protected from the storm by its broad back they were less aware of the angry wind.

The airplanes had gone; there was only a faint rumble far in the distance. The German cannons continued to pound away for a while yet, but finally they, too, fell silent.

All that was left now was the blustering voice of the relentless storm. It roared like a raging monster; and seemed intent on blowing them from the face of the earth.

Storm clouds over the Netherlands. Storm clouds over the whole of Europe. And high above, through the eery darkness of the night and the violence of the storm, slid the Allied bombers, carrying death and destruction to Germany.

The biting wind cut right through their clothes, and Mr. Mulders shivered. He should have put on his overcoat, he thought, but still he didn't move, because the wind, however bone chilling, carried with it a faint, indefinite fragrance that meant the coming of spring.

Mulders knew that there was probably some pretty rough weather ahead in the next weeks, but despite the force of the storm, spring was coming. In fact, this very storm seemed to announce the coming of spring.

It gave him new courage. Just as sure as God kept His promise that spring would follow winter, liberation would come.

Mulders thought about what he had heard about persecutions, arrests and death sentences. He thought about the thousands of people who had been condemned to concentration camps, about the hundreds of thousands of Jews who had been transported to Poland, never to return again. He also thought about the fugitives, spirited away to dark, un-

seen places and secret shelters throughout the country. He thought about Jaap Roseboom, Janus Van Beveren and his wife. There was already so much misery, so much anguish, and Hitler's yoke was becoming more vicious, more deadly every day. What was left of their freedom?

But with despair and doubt came hope and faith. Would the people see this war as an occasion to turn back to God in repentance? If these dark times forced them to their knees, then God would surely send His strength and blessing. Yes, faith enabled you to see the horror and injustice in this war, but it also provided hope.

"Come on, let's go in, we'll freeze out here," he said resolutely.

Back in the house it was warm and light. Mulders and his son moved their chairs closer to the stove to expel the cold from their bones.

A little later he sat down at the small pedal organ in the living room. He went through a repertoire of old, familiar songs and hymns. The others sang along with feeling and conviction.

They ended the evening by asking for God's protection during this cold, stormy night and for deliverance from Nazi tyranny. Then they all went to bed.

Gradually the storm died down. The heavy cloud cover broke, and one tiny patch of dark blue sky became visible. It was enough to show a single bright star—a solace to the suffering and a promise of hope for tomorrow.

The Scout series by Piet Prins:

The Secret of the Swamp

Tom and his friends overhear German military secrets. The secret trail through the swamp puts Scout's talents and Tom's courage to the test.

The Haunted Castle

The mystery of the haunted castle, a coded message hidden under a tree, a gang of smugglers that can vanish at will, a burglary without clues—they all come together when Tom and Scout stumble over a four-hundred-year-old secret.

The Flying Phantom

What connection is there between a dangerous poacher, a police cap on top of a tower, a host of unsolved burglaries, and a mysterious fire?

The Sailing Sleuths

After a confrontation with a gang of carnival followers, Tom and his two friends find themselves wanted by the police.

Titles by Piet Prins:

The Curse of Urumbu

Jack Westerbaan is a Dutch immigrant to Australia. His father's execution by the Germans during World War II put a severe strain on Jack's faith. While in Australia, working as a cowhand, he abandons his faith.

He decides to retrace his roots, but first he wants to cross the continent once more and visit places he's never seen before.

On his journey he kills a wallaby, not knowing he has thereby violated an aboriginal taboo. The tribe's witch doctor pronounces a curse on Jack and the hunt is on.

The story is fast-moving and exciting. Jack's flight lands him in one predicament after another.

Yet this is not action pure and simple; the story is laced with vivid, graphic descriptions of the fascinating Australian landscape.

Run, Kevin, Run!

Orphaned and feeling shipwrecked, Kevin Robbins ends up with relatives who, unlike his own parents, are practising Christians. Unable to make the adjustment, Kevin "cops out" by running away to his home town.

On the way he is adopted by two crooks who insist on "protecting" him from the police. He fools himself into believing that as long as he has no proof of his partners' crimes his own conscience is clear.

Eventually the proof comes. Suddenly Kevin really finds himself wanted by the police. Not knowing where to go, his description broadcast by the media, he drifts aimlessly, intent only on avoiding human contact.

He runs from his mother's memory, from his foster parents, from people who want to help him, from the crooks, from the police. But mostly he runs from himself, accompanied only by another vagabond, Hobojo, his one and only friend.

The Four Adventurers Meet the Evil Professor

When four high school boys decide to spend their summer vacation touring the country in a horse-drawn carriage, they meet up with plenty of action and a whole series of exciting adventures. But their team spirit and a brave, old nag named Skippy carry the boys through one crisis after another.

Tension mounts as Skippy is stolen and then later the hackney is taken by thieves. The boys have a brief encounter with the police, and a confrontation with a dark, sinister character by the name of Professor Pokanini.

The climax occurs when the boys are caught in a frenzied brawl in a barn and are forced to fight for their lives.

The Mystery of the Three-Fingered Villain

As they settle into the cottage on the Overlaar estate for their summer vacation, the four friends—Paul, Roger, Herb and Eddie—look forward to a peaceful summer vacation of swimming, biking, hiking, and taking riding lessons on Skippy, Baron Rensdale's prize horse.

The first few days, however, bring them slashed tires, a mysterious prowler, and a deliberately set grassfire. Paul suspects the events to be related, and soon the four friends are scouring the estate for clues. Their search turns up a road map which they lost on their way to the Overlaar estate and a three-fingered glove.

Their detective work leads to a desperate cross-country chase to rescue their old friend from the three-fingered villain.

The Lonely Sentinel

A windmill standing guard over Dutch polders; the miller's family wrestling with death and treachery; innocent children playing adult games of secrecy and intrigue; hapless refugees hounded by a merciless predator; the men of the Resistance, alert and dedicated . . . often to the death.

Against them, the Hun and his Nazi-sympathizers.

In the balance: Religion, Freedom and the House of Orange . . .

Journey through the Night
by Anne DeVries

After the second world war, Anne DeVries, Holland's most popular novelist, was commissioned to capture in literary form the spirit and agony of those five harrowing years of Nazi occupation. The result was *Journey through the Night,* a four volume bestseller that has gone through more than 30 printings in the Netherlands. This series, which appeals to young and old, is now available in English translation:

> Volume 1 *Into the Darkness*
> Volume 2 *The Darkness Deepens*
> Volume 3 *Dawn's Early Light*
> Volume 4 *A New Day*

Anne DeVries was a prolific writer in many fields. His most concentrated efforts were reserved for children and juvenile literature of which *Journey through the Night* is the first to appear in English translation. Before becoming a full time writer, Anne DeVries was a school teacher.

*"An Old Testament profes-
sor of mine who bought the
books could not put them
down—nor could I."*
— Dr. Edwin H. Palmer

*"This is more than just a
war-time adventure. The
characters have vitality,
depth and great humanity."*
— The Ottawa Citizen

Titles by Meindert DeJong:

Meindert DeJong was born in Wierum, a Frisian village in the Netherlands, and came to the United States when he was eight years old. The DeJong family settled in Grand Rapids, Michigan, where Mr. DeJong grew up and was educated.

In 1962 Mr. DeJong was the first American to be awarded the Hans Christian Andersen Medal by the International Board on Books for Young People.

Dirk's Dog, Bello

The stormy day an English ship broke up in the terrible waters of the Wicked Wife, Dirk rescued the Great Dane, Bello. After that, by the law of the sea, the giant dog belonged to him. Wildly happy at first the boy was suddenly faced with the enormous problem of how to keep Bello, how to feed him—for Dirk's mother was unable to do more than provide for her little family. Dirk's desperate struggles, pathetic and amusing by turns, are the core of this book.

However, this isn't merely the story of Dirk and Bello, but also of a little village in Holland. It is a picture of Wierum itself, the sky, the sea, the dikes, the people—of Aage the Roamer, of Old Ott and her endless prophecies, of the children, the school master, Sipke the village simpleton who played such strange wild music on his accordion, of vast Dikke Trien, and of Mighty Pier. A rare and moving book, full of humor and reality.

Far Out the Long Canal

The award-winning author of *The Wheel on the School, Tower by the Sea,* and other beloved classics has written still another memorable and powerful story about the Netherlands.

In the village of Wierum, at the edge of the North Sea, practically everyone could skate except the very littlest children . . . and Moonta Riermersma, who was already nine years old. When ice finally came to the ditches and canals, Moonta was afire with enthusiasm, not only to learn to skate, but to let his skates lead him on to adventure. And when he heard of something called the New Church's Pipe, far out the long canal, he was determined to find it at any risk.

The action has a magic excitement, and all the characters—Moonta, Mother, Father, Grandfather, Aunt Cora, and the headmaster—are as real as they are appealing. The pictures by Nancy Grossman seem to blow the very winds of Holland right across the pages.